# The

# Next

# Year?

by John Faraday.

Maps and sketches by Alan Faraday.

# The Author:

John Faraday was born in Bootle, Merseyside in 1949, and brought up there and in Southport. He has lived in the North-West of England most of his life, with short spells in Leeds, Sierra Leone and London.

More recently he has visited, lectured and formed friendships with many people in Pakistan, particularly in the Lahore district and in Karachi.

He has three sons and is a keen supporter of a Merseyside football team.

He currently lives in Manchester.

## Author's notes:

I acknowledge the help of special people who have cooperated to make this book possible:

My wife, Joan,
for her loving, consistent help and guidance.

All the family for their patience,
and especially our son Alan,
for his maps, drawings and cover design.

Pete Scanlon and David Pawson
for their invaluable expertise.

My many friends in England and Pakistan
for their friendship and advice.

# Chapter 1. January.
# The Beginning of the End...

JID wanted more to life.

He seemed to have everything. He had a well-paid job in the sales department of Mechanica. He was good at his job. He was a clear thinker and was convinced that he could win a fortune on the 'Shootafact' quiz game if he took the trouble to try. Like all citizens of Northwesteurope (NWE) he could easily travel to any part of the country in a short time. He exercised at home and kept himself in good shape.

But he felt that he was going nowhere and achieving nothing. He felt that the women he met were unable to match his drive and his intellect.

A few months earlier Mighty Malc Mitchum, the managing director of Megatrade, had gone on screen advertising a Special Weekend Event for anyone who was interested. "This weekend will fill up every gap in your life" beamed Mighty Malc, with the usual glint in his eye and a smile that seemed to vary between calm reassurance and a smirk. "This weekend will, in a way that none will have imagined previously, fill you with new feelings, thoughts and sensations as the Programme deals with each person for what he or she is - an individual! Our psychosympathetic Programme will add something extra special to *your* life."

JID had scratched his head and thought deeply (a lot more deeply than most of the shallow minded people around him usually did.) 'Could I really trust Mighty Malc and his empire?' he thought. 'Was there a snag to avoid? Would it be worth the fee? Would it affect his life - and would it be for better or worse?' Eventually he decided that since his life left a lot to be desired anyway, he might as well join in. Perhaps the gorgeous girl of his dreams might just turn up there!

JID eventually signed up for the weekend not quite knowing what to expect - considering that it was such a big event there seemed to be very few details released. Friday, January $2^{nd}$ arrived and he got the correct transport to Liverpool. It was, surprisingly, delayed so he arrived at the door with just a few minutes to spare and there were very few of the 5,000 seats vacant.

Before he could say a word, the secretary at the impressive desk by the entrance, dressed in Megatrade colours said, "Hello, You must be James Ian Davies, JID to your friends. I hope the delay didn't upset you. Can I just check - You are currently single, intelligent and a thinker? You enjoy puzzles and intelligence-type games like chess?"

JID was surprised that a woman who had never seen him before knew so much about him, but for a long time he had suspected that the big companies knew every time you sneezed. The receptionist gave him a badge with his name on and told him to go to floor eight, then through door 14. He took the lift to floor eight and saw about 50 doors at intervals of about three metres to the right of a long corridor. He went into door 14 expecting to be in a small office, but went through a short corridor and through another door that led him to the main arena, decked out in Megatrade's colours. There were a few seats by the aisle, but he picked one next to a beautiful blonde girl about his own age.

"Is it OK if I sit here?" asked JID. She replied "OK", apparently shyly. JID started to talk about being a Junior Director of Mechanica. This was a huge exaggeration, but she would not realise that! They chatted freely. JID explained about his hobbies, work and other matters of interest - all suitably embellished for the hearing of his blond neighbour. He never admitted that one of his favourite pastimes was chess. Instead he talked about enjoying extreme sports, and that he was entering the National Sky Diving Championship.

The girl's badge said her name was Mitty. She said she hated chess, but enjoyed quizzes. ('Near enough', thought JID.) Since the floods she had lived in Liverpool, just two kilometres from the arena. JID explained that he lived in Northampton, 200 kilometres away. The conversation flowed happily so JID was beginning to enjoy the weekend already!

Things seemed to be going well for JID, but suddenly the whole arena, which had been alive with fevered conversation, went silent. JID looked up and there, on the stage and on the huge 3Dvid screens was the unmistakable figure of Mighty Malc, almost 2 metres tall and thin as a rake, clean shaven and with coloured glasses.

"Hello, friends", he roared.

"Hello, Mighty Malc", the adult audience replied with the discipline of schoolchildren at their assembly, but with much more enthusiasm.

"Megatrade is happy to welcome you to their special weekend - your special weekend! This is a weekend just for you!" JID never knew what to make of the smarmy Mighty Malc, but he was giving him a chance.

"Lots of people have asked about the detailed contents of this weekend, but all we could say is that the weekend will be specially designed for the customer, opening your eyes and minds to new events and possibilities."

JID's eyes and mind drifted again to Mitty, who was now snuggling close to him. Perhaps Megatrade, which had so much information about him, had somehow planned that he would come late and spot her next to a spare seat, then form a friendship. Was this what the Programme was all about? Did the companies actually have a human side?

"The Programme we have developed", droned Mighty Malc, "can provide experiences just for you." JID put his arm around Mitty and gave her a squeeze. He was beginning to like this Programme. Mitty smiled and moved even closer.

Suddenly there was a loud sound of scuffling from the doors behind JID. "Everybody remain calm," said Mighty Malc in a reassuring tone. We sometimes get mindless protests at these events - nothing beyond our trusty security people!"

Everyone in the area looked back in trepidation. A group of thugs in the uniform of Shopafrolic burst through the doors and overpowered the doormen. They marched down the steps to JID on the third row and grabbed him. Mitty shouted, "I love you, JID", but they pushed her out of the way. JID placed a few well aimed punches, but they soon overpowered him with the help of a powerful electrode, which paralysed him. He could still see, hear and feel all that was going on, but he couldn't control his muscles. He was trembling violently.

The Shopafrolic gang frogmarched him up to the door, out of the building and past several immobilised Megatrade guards. JID was bundled into the back of a vehicle and driven away. As the vehicle raced along the roads, every movement was agony to JID, who was in the luggage compartment, unable to move his limbs, clattering against the sides of the vehicle as it screeched round corners.

They reached their destination and drove into an empty vehicle park. They then dragged JID by the feet through several doors and into a dark room, where he was dumped for what seemed like several days, although he had no clear way of estimating time. He slept, he woke and spent long hours suspended between the two.

He was hungry, sick and headachy, but he realised that he was beginning to be able to move and realised that feeling was returning. He gingerly started to exercise his very stiff limbs. After a long while he became mobile, but he was still locked up in the dark, and was frightened. He felt around for furniture, but there was nothing except the smelly, soiled mattress he had been lying on. He fumbled around trying to get a better idea of his situation. The room was tiny, just over two metres in each direction. The walls seemed to be off-white, but light squeezed through a small gap around the door. He tried to open the door, but it was firmly locked. He was stark naked.

JID flopped back onto the mattress, trying to gather his thoughts, remembering his trip to Liverpool and Mitty, his new found friend, who had looked on with horror as he was abducted from the arena. He had been kidnapped, and he had no idea why.

There was a rumbling sound and the door opened inwards. He rushed to the door, but bounced off a glass partition. He looked through and saw a kindly looking man, but he was in a Shopafrolic uniform.

"Hello, I'm Kenneth Kippam, a senior officer of Shopafrolic. I do hope our operatives were not too harsh."

JID snapped back "I was attacked, beaten, paralysed, locked in a dark, cold room and half starved by your animals."

He then realised that for some reason Shopafrolic may have been trying to get more information from him. He was also in danger of being punished for saying the wrong thing. He could think of no reason why this may be the case, but he didn't want to take any chances. Were they trying to trap him or his friends and family?

"James Ian Davies," said Kenneth with a kindly tone. "Can I call you JID, everyone else seems to."

JID said nothing. There was silence for a few seconds.

"I must apologise for the actions of our staff. They can be a bit too enthusiastic for their work at times. I do not think that you are a violent man", continued

Kenneth "so we no longer need this glass protection - though for your own safety, I must warn you that we have parasense electrodes available if you try to chance your hand and escape."

Kenneth pressed a button and the glass wall slid silently upwards. "I'd like you to join me for dinner. I understand that your favourite meal is medium-rare steak with chips and mixed vegetables followed by fruit salad, all washed down with a half of Timbros Best." He clicked his fingers and a smart-looking thirty-something lady in uniform came in to take the order. She didn't seem at all surprised that Kenneth had a naked, dirty youth in the office.

"You must be embarrassed dressed like that. I'll bring you some clothes", said Kenneth. He put a well-pressed pile of clothing on a chair. Kenneth saw that it was a Shopafrolic uniform. JID refused to wear it but put on a pair of underpants and a shirt from the pile.

"You probably do not trust me to feed you without poisoning you, so you have the first choice of each dish and I will take the other.

JID was famished and needed no encouragement to eat.

"Tell me about yourself," said Kenneth. "I know most of it already, but what made you apply for the Megatrade weekend? I know you actually have grave misgivings about Megatrade, and you are right! You may consider yourself mistreated, but I have to inform you that, if we hadn't rescued you from Megatrade, you would have been much worse off! I know that you are an individualist - you refuse to fit into anybody's standard profiles. You are above average intelligence. You are shy of girls, but are not homosexual. You do your job conscientiously, but are not especially enamoured by it. We have most of what we need to know about you. But what made you apply for the Megatrade weekend? Don't you suspect all they stand for, like 90% of the population?

"At least Megatrade do not capture people for no reason and..." JID thought for a moment, then said "Look, prisoners of war are only expected to give their name, rank and number. I am James Ian Davies. I am not a member of any armed force, so I have no rank or number. I insist on being released and compensated immediately."

"If only it were so simple," said Kenneth. "You are here for your own protection. Do you realise what Megatrade had planned for you and some of the other innocents in that Liverpool shindig? If I were to explain it, firstly, the very thought of it would terrify the life out of you. Secondly, you probably wouldn't believe it."

Kenneth continued his careful wooing of JID's senses, but JID's mind was alive with questions he dared not ask.

'Is Kenneth who he said he is?' was JID's first thought. 'Is he really acting for Shopafrolic? After all, the event had been planned by Megatrade and introduced by their inimitable, internationally-famous managing director in person. Would they be clumsy enough to let Shopafrolic 'troops' into the building if they hadn't planned it? Perhaps Shopafrolic and Megatrade were really part of the same global corporate monstrosity? The number of multinational companies had reduced to just eight in the last few years and each one was much more powerful than any Government! Had these two nightmare monsters combined to create something even worse? Whatever the real identity of Kenneth and his henchmen, why were they acting in this way? What had he ever done to upset either organisation? Sure, he looked on them with a lot of scepticism, unlike a lot of people who seemed to blindly let it all happen. But why subject him to this?'

Kenneth had continued to speak all this time, but JID did not take anything in. "You seem to have lost track of my argument," smiled Kenneth. "No matter, we can discuss it more fully in the days ahead."

JID recoiled at the thought of being held captive for days by whoever it was, but he was determined to say no more to them. His resolve would match Kenneth's trickery.

"You are not a prisoner," said Kenneth, "although we cannot afford to let you go just now - for your own safety, of course". JID just thought that was corporate double-speak. "However," continued Kenneth, "we will of course treat you well. We will provide a comfortable, large room with 3Dvid-screen and computer, although we cannot allow you to have any contact with the outside world, or Megatrade would track you down."

'What did the liar mean by that', thought JID once again. 'What had he ever done to cause such fear in the companies?'

Kenneth rambled on, "We know which foods you like and which Televids you watch. You are in safe hands and you can relax. You will have a chess set, and internet connection to shopafrolicworld.co.nwe. I regret that we cannot let you use any other site or email. You can play any games you like on the computer, and several of our staff are chess players and will give you a game. This will be like a 6* hotel, to be enjoyed. Please go out of this door, along the corridor and through the second door on the right where you will find your room. Have a shower and relax."

JID passed the first door and saw a stairwell on the left. He decided to take his chance and ran down the stairs. On turning the corner of the stairs he found himself face to face with one of the thugs who captured him in the first place. He aimed a baton and broke one of JID's ribs. Other guards arrived, dragged him to his '6*' room and dumped him on the bed. JID was coughing and spluttering when a medical team arrived, dressed in white but with Shopafrolic logos. They gave him pain killing drugs and one of the team put on Medivision spectacles. He looked at JID's midriff, smiled and said, "Don't worry, JID. There is no great damage apart from the broken rib. Just take it easy for a while. We will give you Vibroweld treatment for three days and that should fix it.

Vibroweld had revolutionised orthopaedic treatment over the last few years, but could he trust this team? However he was still in pain, greatly weakened and partly drugged so he was in no position to object. Once the Vibroweld radiator was turned on JID felt its healing begin and these fears melted away.

"Now relax for a while. Call us if you need us and we will come running," said the chief medic. He looked around nervously then whispered, "Try not to upset the Order Brigade. You are one of the lucky ones- you survived."

The medical team went out and left JID with still more questions.

Meals came and went at what JID assumed were normal times, but, with no sight of daylight and the computer clock disabled he had no way of telling. Each day was punctuated by meals, Vibroweld and a couple of chess opponents. He was careful about what he said to his opponents. He refused to talk about anything that really mattered. When they talked about their family, work, where they lived or people they knew JID heard alarm bells. Were they trying to get information from him? His 'friends' tried to reassure him that they were not part of any interrogation team and that as far as they knew there was no intention to interrogate him. They, like Kenneth, said they were there for his own protection.

JID followed Northampton Town, which had recently been promoted from the Premiership to the NWE Superleague. They had been second to Preston North End. When one of his opponents mentioned football JID asked how Northampton got on. "I could tell you', he replied. JID groaned inwardly. Even the football result was being kept from him.

"...but," continued the opponent, "if you like I can get a 3Dvid and let you see for yourself. There have been three matches since you came here." JID cheered up slightly and accepted.

JID realised that he must have been there for more than a week. Before the opponent left the room 3Dvid coins were delivered to the room, which had the matches on. He was glad that he could see the games, but his fears about being under permanent scrutiny were all proved correct.

Later JID watched the first game. Northampton, in the colours of Mechanica, got a creditable 2-2 home draw against Manchester United which played in the purple and blue of Shopafrolic. After the match the commentators said that United had slipped to second behind Tranmere Rovers, which had beaten Liverpool 3-0 in front of a crowd of 82,000 at New Prenton.

In the Wednesday match, Northampton were playing London United away. Arsenal, Tottenham, Chelsea and

Fulham had combined two years earlier. Northampton won 2-0 to put London into the relegation zone. The gate of 22,400 was London's second highest of the season.

Despite the diversion of chess, football and the Shopafrolic website, time dragged for JID. Each day seemed to last a decade. The next Saturday saw Northampton lose 2-0 to Merziblu at Newison Park, and the next Tuesday Northampton had no game as the larger clubs took part in WHIFL. (The Western Hemisphere International Football League.)

Kenneth Kippam's efforts to get more information from JID increased and varied. Kenneth and JID's chess opponents were like the 'good-cops' who spoke gently to the prisoner. Twice his room was invaded by the lunatic fringe, who gave him a beating. While they gave no further large injuries, he received bruises each time and, each time Kenneth burst in and told the henchmen to behave better towards the guests and told them they had gone too far. After the second visit Kenneth clapped his hands and another paramilitary came with a parasense electrode, which he used on the most violent of his colleagues.

"You see," said Kenneth, "I have no hostile intentions against you personally. I must check who let them into your room. He, too, will be suitably punished."

"I met your older brother at a party last week," said Kenneth. "He's quite a personality, isn't he? He told me about his research work on Psychleads. They will do the job of parasense, but much more effectively. You must be impressed by him.

JID didn't have an older brother, but he decided to play along. "He was the rat who always stole my toys and criticised my school work. I got my own back the day I pushed him off the top board in the swimming pool. He fell flat on his back and was in hospital for a week. That gave me the chance to tell him a few home truths. He never pushed me around again, although my parents gave me a hard time for a month or two. He then became as bad, worse than the peole who use parasense, trying to make a more painful one."

"You liar" roared Kenneth. "You haven't got an older brother."

"I am no more a liar than the one who said I have got a brother."

"It was a psychological test of your personality. Now why not try to be friendly and we will be able to speak honestly and openly."

"I am James Ian Davies. I am not a member of any military force so I have no military rank or number." He then stopped talking to Kenneth despite Kenneth's efforts to have a conversation.

Kenneth left, but about 20 minutes later, while JID was waiting for his evening meal, he was startled by a series of crashing sounds. (He wasn't sure, but he thought he heard some gun shots.) The noise was getting nearer, and his door burst open to reveal a stormtrooper in a Megatrade uniform. "Hey, Burt," he yelled, "I think I've found one of the kids captured by Shopafrolic!"

The commander came into the room. "Relax, we've come to rescue you", he said.

JID didn't know what to believe.

The commander continued, "In a few minutes we will have defeated the opposition. Stay here for now then we will come and take you to freedom."

'What kind of freedom will THIS be?' wondered JID.

The noise of battle continued for a few minutes and then all went quiet. JID did not know which uniform he would see next, but it was Burt, carrying a spare Megatrade uniform. "Here, put this on and we will take you to the debriefing session before your complete freedom.

They walked down some steps and JID saw daylight for the first time through the window. It was snowing. JID didn't want to wear any uniform (especially a Megatrade uniform in Shopafrolic premises) but under the circumstances there seemed no choice as he would soon be outside in the elements. He was put in the back of a comfortable transport pod and taken a few blocks. As he passed the Livershop building, with the Liver Birds on top he realised that he was in Liverpool near the arena. The Livershop Company, which had been founded in 2010 claimed that it had invented the

Liver Bird as its logo when they built the building. The huge Liver Bird statues had in fact been in place since the 1930s. Hundreds of people were approaching the arena from all directions, a few on foot, but most in transport. He recognised some people that he had seen when he first went to the arena, and wondered if Mitty would be there.

At reception the same receptionist he had seen previously spotted him and said, "Hello, Mister Davies, floor eight, door 14 again." Then she promptly started dealing with the next person.

On entering the door he was surprised to find the corridor transformed into a changing room and his own clothes were clean, pressed and hung up ready to wear.

On one of two comfortable seats was a sexy secretary who beckoned him to sit down on the other. He sat, and she started abusing Shopafrolic. "Now for your debriefing," she said, and then giggled, apparently at the double entendre.

JID was not prepared to say anything and all she could get was his usual, well-practised, "I am James Ian Davies. I am not a member of any armed force, so I have no rank or number. I insist on being released and compensated immediately."

The secretary smiled and said, "I suppose I cannot blame you for being cagey after what Shopafrolic did to you, but I really am your friend…." and she continued unsuccessfully to try to speak to him. Eventually she gave up and said, "It's time for the final meeting soon. Do not get changed just yet, until you have attended the final meeting. Please enter the auditorium."

He went through the other door into the auditorium. His heart sank when he looked across the auditorium to see Mitty kissing and cuddling with someone else. He took the first available seat and waited for the event to start. He glanced at the faces of the other participants. Some were overjoyed. Some anxious. Some perplexed. Some in pain. Some seemed high on various kinds of drugs.

Mighty Malc appeared on stage and screen. Everyone seemed overjoyed at his presence, but JID thought they were all far too gullible. The cheer grew to a crescendo, lasting several minutes until Mighty Malc held up a hand and everyone was instantly quiet, again acting like well-trained children.

A shout split the air - "We adore you, Mighty Malc". It was a woman in her mid-thirties, suitably uniformed like everyone else. Another roar hit the air as everyone (except JID) expressed their appreciation of the woman's remark.

Mighty Malc held up his hand again and this time it was he who broke the silence. "Have you had a worthwhile weekend?" he asked, and the whole hall roared "Yes" in unison.

'This was much longer than a weekend!' thought JID.

"Was it enlightening?"

"Yes."

"Will it benefit you in the years ahead?"

"Yes."

"Are you impressed with Megatrade?"

"Yes."

"...and who inspires Megatrade?"

"Mighty Malc! Mighty Malc! Mighty Malc! Mighty Malc!" they chanted.

JID sat with his head in his hands as the others seemed to be in a trance. He then realised that others were casting disapproving glances at his non-compliance, so, with a heavy heart, he began to shout "Mighty Malc! Mighty Malc!"

Mighty Malc thanked the audience and asked if anyone would like to say what had happened. Several people went to the microphone telling a wide variety of stories, from the very good to the very bizarre. Each ended with a heartfelt tribute to Mighty Malc and Megatrade.

Mighty Malc then said, "Some of you had a more difficult time. We hadn't planned for Shopafrolic thugs to break in and kidnap people! Would one of you like to come forward to say what happened?"

JID stormed out of his seat in row ZZ determined to show the whole event to be a farce, but a man in his forties on the second row easily got there first. "I was captured by Shopafrolic people two days ago. I had always thought that Big Business had the best interest of all the population, but Shopafrolic proved me wrong. It is so reassuring that we have benevolent organisations like Megatrade."

He continued to describe his experiences, which were very similar to JID's. He apologised to Mighty Malc, the board and staff of Megatrade and everyone present for being fooled by Kenneth Kippam of the Shopafrolic intelligence service. "Now", he declared with the apparent joy of the penitent, "I have seen the truth after my rescue by the fine men of Megatrade."

The crowd erupted in loud cheers, and they stood as one in applause at this speech. Only JID remained seated. If he tried to put the other side of the question he would probably be lynched! Surely, he thought, the event took much more than two days. Surely others would soon realise that. Surely they would soon go public and show the event for what it was, and save other people from going down the same mind-bending path. JID lived in hope.

After the meeting JID was delighted to be able to put on his own clothes and dump the Megatrade uniform, but, as he walked away from the arena, he was disturbed to see that almost everyone was still in uniform and many had even left their own clothes behind.

Could he ever be sure that his version of the event was right? Was he the one who had suffered from illusions? Had it all happened in one crazy weekend?

He got to the transport link and had a wait of about three minutes before he could board for Northampton. He turned on his Contactaworld and said, "Football Results."

The Contactaworld said "Here are the NWE Superleague results for 24$^{th}$ and 25$^{th}$ January..."

# Chapter 2. February.
# The Demise of the Airports...

"Heathrow Airport has had a fascinating history", roared the Prime Minister to the enraptured audience. 93% of the adult population watched the live TV broadcast as she addressed Parliament. "Indeed, without Heathrow Britain would have been seriously hindered in many ways and would not have been able to take its lead in so many of the achievements of the last century. This country (and indeed so much of the developed world) was devastated by the 1939 to 1945 war, but people of vision and understanding helped this country to rise from the ashes. The skills and abilities developed in wartime were applied to peaceful purposes. We excelled in them and the benefits were made available to all. But Heathrow Airport..." (she paused for effect) "has now served... its purpose!" (Her voice rose to a Churchillian crescendo, before continuing more quietly). "The other Terminals have been put to good use. Only Terminal 3 remains.

"The Health Service made medical treatment available to each person in our land. The National Rail Service made internal transport quicker and easier than it had ever been, coupled with the vast road-building operation that made it possible for goods and people alike to reach each corner of this land, while the air industry reached the other side of the globe in hours.

"Our Empire became a commonwealth of free, friendly nations and all benefited. Transport, through great international hubs like this very airport, brought nations of the world so much closer. This airport was an important part of that link between Northwesteurope and the world! We are at the centre of that important link." The Prime Minister paused for effect. There was a ripple of loud applause in the auditorium and some cheering could be heard in most corners of the nation, then she continued, "Heathrow Airport was a hub for the movements of Presidents and Prime Ministers, singers and sports stars, footballers and financiers, bishops and businessfolk, immigrants and emigrants, technologists and travellers.

"Most of the airport is already being re-used well. Heathrow became great in the last century, and we want it to best satisfy the thoughts and desires, indeed the aspirations of the millions who have moved out from London- and the ones who have bravely decided to remain there. It will become part of the memory of and memorial to those who helped to make London great before the floods and earthquakes that devastated the city.

"Terminal 1 was developed for luxury housing while people still desired to live in London. The project was so successful that these flats are still enjoyed by those who live there, and they appreciate the swimming pools, squash courts and amenities that give the privacy of home with the amenity of a leading hotel. The people on the west side of Terminal 1 enjoy a perfect view of the beautiful countryside, while those on the east side get free views of London United's new stadium, just below them, as part of the deal.

"Terminal 2 is now a major research establishment. Our nation continues to lead the world at the very cutting edge of science and technocracy! We also provide the best scientific centres on Earth and so scientists from many nations come to enjoy our facilities and combine with others, led by prominent Northwesteuropeans, to tackle the few questions that are still unanswered by the human race. Even the best universities on our planet are unable to match the standard of facilities and the intellect that are both so clearly seen in Terminal 2.

"Heathrow became great during the 20th century and the start of the 21st century. The hard working Airport-Use Planning Committee has now completed its work apart from dotting the final I's and crossing the final T's. Terminal 5 has become a museum of the 20th century. That was the century when London achieved most and became the symbol of excellence that most of the world tried, largely unsuccessfully, to emulate. London was the centre of world trade, culture, sport, architecture, education, research, engineering and so much more." The PM gave extra stress to the word 'more' almost musically.

"As we all know, Heathrow Airport is no more. The final jet flight from Terminal 3 has flown, leaving us with important decisions to be made. How should these buildings be used? The value of the land is now so low that, sadly, no self-respecting financier would take the terminal as a gift! The cost of converting or replacing the buildings would be many times the value of the land or the likely profit available.

"Despite the problems your Government faced and in consultation with our financier Mr. Oscar Victor of Shopafrolic, we have found a solution that would solve all the related problems at one stroke. Should Parliament agree, Mr. Victor has offered to turn Terminal 3 into an Aviation Theme Park. Visitors will be able to enjoy joining baggage queues! They will be able to buy old-style paper passports and these 'passengers' will be checked, x-rayed and frisked for weapons, and will be able to buy duty free goods. They will be able to sit in control towers and learn to safely control planes from 1950s onwards - Comets to Boeing 878s - on computers that are elaborate even by today's exacting standards. They will be able to 'pilot' planes, serve refreshments or be passengers. They will be able to try handling and organising the many tons of luggage that passed through here. They will even be able to be members of virtual fire crews for when planes have virtual crashes. These machines are so reliable and advanced that those involved will feel the heat of the fire and smell the fuel. Nothing will be left to the imagination. If this scheme is approved by Parliament it will bring much needed employment to this poor corner of Northwesteurope.

"We move forward strongly, in confidence of a better future for our great nation, appreciating the moral, financial and intellectual support of the people. I give you Terminal 3."

Jean Brett, the Prime Minister sat down with loud applause coming from all sides of the House. Like all parliamentary debates for several years it was a foregone conclusion. There were no other speeches for or against, no questions and no further details of the scheme given. The house divided with 477 members supporting the motion. 17 opposed, (there were always some who were told to oppose to give the appearance of democracy) and the remaining 35 were elsewhere on 'official business'. 'Official business' was the Government's description of MPs who had previously voted against measures when they were not invited to. This 'official business' was permanent.

The media was full of the speech, giving unanimous support to the PM and parliament.

. . . . .

With this speech the gap between reality and public credulity reached a new extreme. All but a tiny minority believed every word that the Prime Minister uttered but the truth was very different.

"Terminal 1 was developed for luxury housing..." she had claimed. Three years earlier she had promised that 85 large luxury flats would be built in Terminal 1. She declared that detailed plans had been drawn up to use every square centimetre of the building. Naturalite bulbs would be used to save people from the eyestrain of normal electric lighting. She had promised that people on one side would have views of natural park areas while those on the other side would have free views of London United's matches. She said that their windows would be 100% soundproof so that they could watch the matches in silence if they wished. Those who lived in any of the flats would have 24 hour room service paid for in advance as part of the purchase price. They could use the gymnasium and other sports facilities free of charge. The shops and other facilities would be exclusively for their use, but with prices as low as any on the High Street.

Terminal 1 was actually a slum with no facilities at all. They had to walk over a kilometre if they needed so much as a plastainer of milk. People on the same side as the football ground could see the game, but heard every word that the crowd chanted through their leaky window frames, despite an earlier promise of soundproof glass in these 'luxury' apartments. People on the other side could see a wasteland of tips and building sites, where the contractors had gone bust years before. The plumbing facilities were inadequate and cholera was common among the children who lived there.

Amazingly, when the PM made big claims about Terminal 1 there was no complaint from the inhabitants. They were taken in as completely as everyone else. It was as if she had been talking about a different time and place.

Terminal 2, the Scientific Centre had become a factory where test tubes and other laboratory equipment were manufactured, but never used. They were taken to the remaining universities for the research to take place. There was a plentiful supply of unskilled labour from Terminal 1, but the pay, and consequently the standard of the product, were rock bottom. The output from the factory had already dropped by 42% from the first year, but that didn't matter - the orders had dropped by 61%.

Amazingly, Terminal 5 was a financially successful venture for the owners, Livershop. Livershop had trading centres in all the major cities and even in some of the smaller ones like London. All these centres successfully overcharged for everything from basic foodstuffs to the most high-tech experienceometries. The success for Livershop never created any real advantage for the customer, but even though the standard of living was diving, people failed to notice.

In Terminal 5, Livershop hadn't opened their usual store, but had gone into their version of culture. In different ways they tried to show that every great development of Northwesteuropean culture, in politics, engineering or art down the ages had been the result of Livershop's beneficent influence - despite their recent foundation! Their claims about founding the Liver Building (now the Livershop Building) in Liverpool was just a reflection of their other claims.

The public had listened intently to the Prime Minister and absorbed every word, however extreme or ridiculous it may have been. Because of the successful mind-numbing techniques of the large companies, with all the Governments of the world in their pockets, they were able to manipulate the public as they wished. Terminals 1, 2, 3 and 5 had been accounted for in Jean Bratt's speech, but what of Terminal 4? Nobody cared or even noticed that it was missing in the speech as their critical ability had been eroded so much. For now the Government simply ignored it in its official statements. At a later date, if it ever became possible to put it to another use it would conveniently reappear - though that could only ever be a dream of the most optimistic politician or mogul!

...or the most gullible 'man-in-the-street', but there were plenty of them around!

. . . . .

Ten years previously a group of South American terrorists had stormed Terminal 4. It was costing a fortune to run each terminal, the amount of international travel was rapidly decreasing as conventional air travel was becoming so expensive.

Even though the flood, with its devastating effect on London, was still two years into the future, Heathrow had one terminal too many. The companies had already had informal talks about how to use Terminal 4 and they were considering an approach to the Government to tell them what to do. Then Megatrade had come up with an idea that would solve all their problems.

Gaucho Gonzales from Mexico had become the scourge of the companies. He was behind a series of high profile attacks on megacompany and Government property in many parts of the world. It was impossible to contain or imprison him as he kept armies all around him. Loyalist commandos formed a solid block half a kilometre around Gonzales' headquarters in Peru, while specialist mercenaries formed a ring further away. On the mountains around he had the most sophisticated rockets and guidance systems, which would immediately disable any missile or plane that got near. He had men who were prepared to risk all to strike a blow at the companies, and they had already taken down oil rigs and refineries, office blocks, docks, factories and other facilities. For Gonzales and his henchmen, the bigger the better. The latest jets from various air forces had been shot down by the Gonzales' organisation. He promised that his utter destruction of the Kremlin was only the start of his actions against world Governments.

The Governments spoke strongly against Gonzales, yet many MPs and representatives who could still think for themselves were secretly glad that Gonzales was around as it seemed that he was the only effective opponent to the companies. While he ran riot, the megacompanies did not have things completely their own way.

The megacompanies, of course, wanted to remove him by fair means or foul. They started a plot to use Terminal 4 as a prison for Gonzales and his gang. They decided that the only way to get Gonzales into the Terminal was to get him to go there voluntarily! There was no way that they would ever be able to capture him on his home turf. Megacompany spies in the Gonzales ranks started to informally suggest that it would be a huge coup for Gonzales to be part of one of the guerrilla gangs, to capture and hold an important building in a western capital. A spy who floated the idea to Gonzales was promoted and made one of his personal advisers. He had the responsibility of planning the whole scheme. The plan took almost a year from its inception. Henriqué Solas became code named G14, and was given a fake Northwesteuropean passcard in the name of Henry Solent. He had four months holiday in Mayfair's Comprehendant Hotel paid for by his other employers, the NWE Parliament, while still receiving a generous allowance from Gonzales! To get any information he needed he only had to ask his NWE contact, while living in luxury. He sent messages to Gonzales about his progress so far and the difficulties he encountered. G14 knew that if he sent the final report to G1 (Gonzales) too soon the NWE plot would be too obvious.

Eventually he sent details of every corridor and storeroom of the whole airport to Gonzales. He also sent false details of the military positions at and near the airport. G1 had asked for these details as they would be so important for his attack.

Eventually Gonzales sent a message via a trusted courier to G14. He sent him a note, handwritten and signed personally, in which he commended G14 for a magnificent piece of subterfuge. He invited G14 to join him at his home for his birthday party the following Wednesday.

Gonzales had several 'birthday parties' each year! Everyone in his employ knew that they were summit meetings of his employees and partners to congratulate and decorate those who had achieved great things, or to finalise important plots. Often, as in this case, he would do both at the same 'party.'

Henry Solent booked out of the hotel and boarded the transport to Lima, where Henriqué Solas was welcomed by G6. They were taken to Gonzales' HQ in the Peruvian Andes in a luxury appartment, and awaited the 'birthday party.' The party went like many parties that well-off people hosted. The host paid for the lavish accommodation and all the food and drinks. There was loud music in one area and quieter rooms where all kinds of social activities, from discussion to prostitution, could take place. There were several gaming rooms where Gonzales offered huge odds in favour of the gambler - all at his own expense.

Henriqué mainly stayed in the quieter rooms, mixing happily and catching up with friends whom he had not seen for months.

After a couple of hours Gonzales had the music turned down and called for silence on the PA system, which was now connected to every corner of the sprawling premises. He called for everyone to come into the ballroom. About 50 loyalists gradually appeared and sat around the dance floor. When Gonzales spotted Henriqué he beckoned him to come forward.

Gonzales spoke to the crowd. As usual he started, "Comrade revolutionaries, you will be surprised to learn that today is not my birthday!" There was a ripple of laughter from regular guests. He continued, "I have several things to say to you, but first I would like to introduce a man I promoted to G Level six months ago. I have not been able to introduce him to you earlier as I sent him on a very dangerous mission from which he has recently returned very successfully. He went to London to get information on Heathrow Airport for our guerrilla attack like no other. Our plan is not to destroy, but to gain part of the airport as a permanent base. This would be impossible without good intelligence. Henriqué Solas, now to be honourably referred to as G14, was one of the men who had the vision for this amazing scheme. After careful discussion with him, I sent him to London with a huge shopping list of information that we needed, carefully committed to his memory as it would be dangerous to put it on paper. He went to London as planned, knowing that capture would lead to certain death. He gradually met people, broke into buildings, kept his eyes open and gathered all the information we required. When he acquired this intelligence he sent it to me via a series of different avenues so that his modus operandi would not be compromised. G14 will also accompany me when I go to Heathrow."

This was a shock to Henriqué. He thought his job was done. He had no desire to be part of the raiding party, even though he already knew that NWE troops could only give symbolic resistance. However, in these circumstances he was in no position to object.

"If all my men had the loyalty, endurance and ability of G14" said Gonzales, "we would be able to take over the world tomorrow. I give you G14!"

The audience all started the rhythmical handclap reserved for Gonzales and those who were special heroes of the revolution, and G14 appreciated the accolade even though he did not appreciate being part of the raiding party.

Henry Solent and other spies sent messages back to London describing how Gonzales had completely fallen for the NWE plan. They would have a couple of NWE troops and various remote devices around T4, to convince Gonzales and his team that the battle was genuine, but let him in with no real fight. He would then become a prisoner at the site that was to have been his greatest triumph. Troops stationed a few hundred metres away would surround the terminal and keep Gonzales out of action. They reckoned that, if he were captured, the whole organisation would crumble.

The NWE plan backfired! Yes, the companies knew every thought and movement of Gonzales. What they (and G14) failed to realise was that Gonzales also had spies at a high level in the NWE parliament and some of the companies. He knew all that they had planned.

Gonzales and his raiding party took off on a Supertour Holiday Jet from Argentina as NWE expected. Henriqué was sitting at a place of honour at the front of the aircraft, across the aisle from Gonzales. Henriqué realised that his safety belt was jammed. He was unable to get up out of his seat, but thought nothing of it at the time. Gonzales saw him struggling with the belt and said, "Don't worry, I'll get someone to fix it later."

About an hour into the flight Gonzales asked for, and received, a microphone from the stewardess. He started by paying tribute to his loyal comrades, and said that this time his birthday had truly arrived! He praised a few of his leaders and then started to talk about G14. "You have all heard my tribute to G14. However, I did not tell you the whole truth. The only way a leader can deal with intelligence correctly is to be more intelligent than the opposition. G14 is not the only man I get intelligence from! I also have loyal men and women in NWE! They told me about his living in luxury and being fed with caviar, and the information NWE chose to send to us. They also sent me the real information that I needed. Where their armies will actually be based… how strong those armies are… their plans to capture me… and so on. I even knew about Solas's idea before he did! My spies in NWE had begun to suggest it three years ago! I knew that NWE were planning to capture me. So my plans are much bigger and better than any of my staff, or the NWE people realise."

Henriqué was now terrified. He knew that Gonzales would have some diabolical scheme planned for him. Gonzales continued his diatribe, "Now I come to the part that NWE does not realise! Twenty minutes and ten minutes before we arrive, a Historiholiday Jet from Peru, and another from Mexico City, will land at Heathrow full of tourists. These tourists are actually my troops, and they will attack the places where we know the NWE forces actually are, not where this creature says they are!" (He pointed to Henriqué and spat in his direction). "We will take their forces by surprise and win a complete victory. We will set up machine gun posts and rocket launchers on Terminal 4 to hold that terminal, and at a radius of several miles against any military activity. Any attack on our stronghold will result in other terminals being blown sky high and planes being permanently grounded. The NWE Government and all the companies will be unable to stop us. They will be forced to allow our intelligence work, our drug-running, our terrorism against strategic centres, and all our work in Europe to be centred there because they will not want the airport area to be devastated. You have your orders. Today will give us a great victory!" The troops on board started the rhythmical handclap.

For the next hour Gonzales sat next to Henriqué and taunted him; then he stood up to address the plane again. "I haven't yet decided what to do with Solas. If any of you would like to do it for me I would be most pleased. I now have another priority," he said as he went towards the toilet. When he returned he glanced at the battered, blood-stained and very dead body of Henriqué, and smiled.

Gonzales's plan worked even better than he expected. His troops were driven by their loyalty and their passion. On the other hand, the brainwashed NWE men knew for whom they were fighting, but had had their desire, intelligence and mental agility weakened a long time previously. They also had no real stomach for the fight as their purpose in life was to toe the line. When NWE suffered surprise attacks at different parts of Heathrow they were given no line to toe. Less than two hours after landing at Heathrow, Gonzales had taken Terminal 4 and killed every NWE soldier within three kilometres.

At the time the Government and the megacompanies had not used their control over the media in a big way, but that all began to change. The news Programmes declared that military manoeuvres had taken place in London. They showed the Prime Minister's speech to Parliament. A younger, leaner Jean Brett had said, "Some people have heard gunshots and explosions over London. There is absolutely no need to be alarmed. We have merely been having practise manoeuvres to keep our forces at the peak of readiness in the event of any attack from opposition from inside or outside of NWE. We planned an attack on Terminal 4 of Heathrow by some of our armed forces, which was opposed by other regiments of our brave men. After this we can have even better confidence in the ability of our forces to keep us all safe. If any of you think that any real harm has been done, why not go along to Terminal 4 and see that all is well there." The TVs cut to show current pictures of Terminal 3. They then showed Terminal 4 operating well at full capacity. The footage they showed was, in fact, three years old and had been shown several times already in different contexts. Nobody noticed that these were old pictures.

After the PM finished her speech with the words, "Because of our brave forces you can sleep in peace and comfort", everybody did!

The population was already conditioned to accept the PM's word as truth. Most took her word as reliable. Some actually went to visit Terminal 4 confident that all was well, and were reassured to see for themselves. Some noticed that the top of Terminal 4 had sprouted some changes in the previous days, but nobody asked why. Some people who had booked flights from Terminal 4 got communications telling them of the changes. They, too, accepted it without asking questions.

. . . . .

All that was ten years ago, but now Heathrow had seen its last flight. Every terminal was, according to the Government, used in the best possible way. Every one of the five Terminals was being effectively used for another purpose- all four of them!

And Gonzales was happily in control of Terminal 4.

# Chapter 3. March.
# The Start of JID's Recovery...

JID had returned home to Northampton feeling a shadow of his former self. He had been determined to return to normality as quickly as possible so that he could put January's events behind him. He had been amazed that, when he returned to work nobody, from the project director to the tea man, had asked him about his time away. His workmates glanced up and said, "Hello" when he walked in, just the same as the last time they saw him. His pay had gone into his bank account on the right day of the month. It was as if nothing had happened.

He continued as he had before but, after a few weeks, the strain of the events of the 'Convention' were beginning to weigh him down and he decided to ask his firm for a break. JID rarely saw the boss, who had a reputation as a clear thinker who knew all that was going on, so JID went, with fear and trembling, to his office, thinking that he would be firmly told that he had had too much time off already. JID was surprised that the boss seemed to be glassy eyed and becoming as vague as a lot of the other people with whom he came into contact. When he asked for time off, the boss glanced up at him. He wasn't wearing the glasses he had always had before and there was no apparent sign of contact lenses. He said, "Sure, you can have as much time off as you like!"

JID could hardly believe what he heard, and said, with a little trepidation, "I won't be punished for taking too much time off? I won't get the sack or lose any pay?"

"No."

"Will you put that in writing?"

"Yes." Then the boss nodded to the secretary who started to type permission for JID to take leave as he desired. The secretary produced the document with three spelling errors and, as far as JID could see, at least two grammatical errors, but the boss duly signed it. JID checked the letter and, apart from the fact that it could have been typed by any eleven year old child, it was unambiguous! He could have his time off.

JID needed to get away from his Northampton home, but not be too close to Liverpool. The only place he could think of (and the only place he could afford) was his parents' home. It was in Preston, the latest place to be formally absorbed into Greater Liverpool, but it was about 50 kilometres north of Liverpool itself and still retained an atmosphere of its own. It was far enough away for JID to feel safe.

His father was a school site manager, with responsibility for making sure that the building was clean, safe and secure. For many years his mother had been a secretary. They had moved to Preston a few years earlier when his father got a similar job for a similar salary, but in and around Preston you could buy property much cheaper, and so they were able to buy their own home for the first time. It was a cosy, 19$^{th}$ Century terraced house.

JID trusted and admired his father, who had always given him sound advice on most things. Like any self-respecting son he did not always follow the advice but he usually regretted it when he didn't. When he arrived, his father poured him a Timbros Best and said, "How are things, James? Have you been doing anything interesting lately?"

JID tried to change the subject. He would discuss the Convention when and if he felt that it was right. He reminded his father, Nigel Davies, that he liked to be called JID, not James any more. He started talking about football. Nigel boasted that Preston North End was doing well in its first season in the NWE Superleague. The conversation went on at this superficial level, and JID felt as if he was a million miles from the horror he suffered at Liverpool a few weeks earlier. He quickly relaxed.

His parents sensed that JID had a lot on his mind and they tried unsuccessfully to get him to talk about whatever was troubling him. He had not talked about the Convention to anyone, not even to his parents. His father saw a lot of him each day, but always went to the Club in the evenings. Nigel and JID's mother, Sarah, wanted him to be able to relax more and thought he may enjoy the Club. They realised that JID would not be pushed into anything new so Nigel invited him to the Club once just to let him know he would be welcome should he decide to come along. He assured JID that there were at least two people with whom he would get on well.

One day he went to his room and switched on the 3Dvid Screen. The Prime Minister made her usual appearance, very convincing to most people, but JID could see right through most of her calm, reassuring presentation. When she had finished she handed over to her, "Very close friend, Joe King ABC - the Archbishop of Canterbury himself."

JID hadn't previously had the patience to listen to any religious talk. He had once heard someone describe school religious information lessons as an injection against religion, to stop you catching the real thing! His injection had worked perfectly. Even so, he wondered if Joe King's philosophy might just give him some way to deal with his Liverpool experience. He suspected not (could a friend of Jean Brett really help him to get a life?) but would give him a try. Perhaps this way of thinking or acting would make all the difference. Did they have some way of life that would be able to give him something extra - that something that would help him to have confidence for the future?

The heavy, over fat frame of Joe King bounced in and made JID jerk to one side as he seemed to be flying towards him out of the 3Dvid screen. "Yes, folks! It's me, Joe King. Joe King by name - joking by nature!" He paused for effect. "Religion is really nice," he enthused, "especially since we have found the best way to think of it. It used to be rules and regulations! But who dare say that adultery is wrong now that I, the ABC, do it so often! Anyway, with the formal ending of marriage we don't have that problem anymore! Mrs. ABC has her own peccadilloes, but what do I care? Stealing is OK provided you do not get caught! This is real religion. At some stage in history religious people have been involved in all of this - and almost all other human behaviour. So I say that we should stop being judgemental! Generally we should try to be nice to people. Even Jesus said something like that!

"This faith that I now proclaim is the only faith that all Governments and major companies endorse." (That comment alone made JID squirm, having suffered so much at the hands of the companies!) "I am a leader of Christianity, but we have leaders from every faith and none. The leader of Worldfaith in India was a Hindu, and in Afghanistan the leader was a Moslem. We have been able to unite faiths by using a different approach to theology. Instead of finding where we differ, we throw away all the differences and cuddly niceness is left behind. You can still pray to God - if you want to!" The ABC looked as if he was trying not to laugh. "But why worry about that kind of thing if you do not want to. You do not need a Greater Being to have a deep spiritual religious experience! THIS religion ignores the differences and unites us in the truth.

"Pope John XXIII wanted to open discussions with people of other faiths. We have done much better in combining with them! Pope Shambolic I, soon to be elected, will declare that the Roman Catholic Church will join Anglicans, Baptists, Hindus, Pentecostal Christians, Moslems and others in the true Worldfaith.

JID heard cheering from the house next door, as well as warm applause from the studio audience, which sat next to him on the 3Dvid.

"This religion will bring true peace to the earth. Someone, I think it was a Moslem, once talked about 'The peace that passeth understanding.' This is what we are working towards. This is being shown to be possible.

"There are problems, however! There are people who want to narrowly define faith! There are people claiming to represent Christianity who think that they are the only people who know the way to true faith. They are dangerous predators like Al Qaeda used to be! What arrogance! These enemies will be hunted down, silenced and if necessary stamped out and religiously cleansed by all means are available to the civilised soldiers of Worldfaith! This is the way to peace!"

The ABC sat down to rapturous applause from the hall where he spoke, from next door to JID and, almost certainly, from most of the people in the country. But JID wondered if he had heard correctly! The ABC had spoken about peace and reconciliation, and then stamping people out in the next breath! Did he really expect or even want to join the rest of the population in an organised hatred that they couldn't even recognise as such? Did he want his mind to be so confused by the current trends that he became completely unable to distinguish between reasonable thought and blind faithlessness. It didn't take him long to conclude that religion was nothing more than another chord in the companies' overwhelming overture of mind control.

He tried to flick on to another channel, but couldn't during the news item. Later there was no football on, so he settled for a 'Tom and Jerry' 2d film on ArchiveTV. He preferred to watch humorous, cartoon violence than listen to the Archbishop threatening his detractors with the real thing.

JID fell asleep, and was wakened by his mother calling that it was time for tea. In all Greater Liverpool, tea meant either a cup of tea or the main meal in the evening. In this case it was a good meal, and JID was soon demolishing it. Her medium rare steak followed by a Timbros always tasted better than anyone else's, and infinitely better than the best that Joe Kippam had produced. After the family meal Nigel got himself ready and went to the Club. JID didn't go, but was beginning to think that he might give it a go soon just to satisfy his growing curiosity. The next day, when Nigel was getting ready to go, JID asked if the invitation was still valid. "Of course," said Nigel.

They walked the few blocks to the Club, and JID was surprised to find that it was a chess club. It was a good thing that he had been a few days with his parents, as an earlier invitation to a chess club would have received a firm 'No' from JID, remembering his long hours playing chess at the premises of Megatrade, or Shopafrolic or whoever it was. A bright side, perhaps the only bright side of his January experiences, was that his chess had greatly improved and he would not make such a fool of himself against the experts.

As they were reaching the Club Nigel made some comments that confused JID even more. He said that if he wanted to describe a knight on the chess board, there were times when it should still be called a knight, but at other times it was a horse.

JID remembered the days of his childhood when his father always told him off for describing the piece as a horse, and grinned. "Why?" He asked.

His father simply said, "Don't worry about that for now! Until you figure it out, call a knight 'that piece'."

Nigel went into the Club followed by JID. The lower floor was square, each outer wall was about thirty metres long. There was a staircase alongside one outside wall. The only other walls on the ground floor surrounded a kitchen in the middle, with a bar on two adjacent sides. The room around the kitchen had a variety of coffee tables and longer tables with an untidy jumble of sofas around the tables. There were several chess boards set out ready to play. There were several people there and some were already playing chess.

Nigel and JID entered. "Hello, Nigel", said a smart looking man a few yards from the door. "Is this the son you told me about?"

JID wondered what they had said about him, but knew his father would not say anything bad about him. "Yes, meet James. James, this is Mark McCallow, who has become a great friend of mine recently. He is a man worth talking to - you may have seen him on the 3Dvid a year or two ago. And his daughter's a beautiful girl!"

That last comment made JID take notice, but he couldn't stop himself potentially making a fool of himself before the father of a beautiful girl by insisting that he was usually called JID. However, this didn't harm his chances as Mark simply said, "Then I will call you JID! Would you like a game?"

Before JID could answer, his father asked, "Are all the knights in place?"

"Yes, four horses, all ready."

Nigel said "Oh, good", and looked immediately more relaxed.

JID was puzzled, but sat down for a game. He had become quite an expert during his time in captivity, but Mark McCallow seemed to be thinking two moves ahead of JID. JID played well, but after half an hour he came to the conclusion that his position was hopeless and resigned. Mark started to play against Nigel while JID watched.

At the Chess Club there were two surprises for JID. The players and spectators chatted freely during the play. Despite their great ability at the game - chess did not seem to be the most important thing - their minds were alert to many other matters. That fact, in itself, made the Club unusual! JID had noticed that so many people were like his boss. Even the most gifted were generally becoming like zombies, with no real interest in anything of importance. Even he, in his early twenties, could remember the days when local and national politics would often cause most people to consider how and why decisions were made and their results on their lives and other peoples', often resulting in heated but generally friendly debate. Now people simply endorsed the power blocks - the companies and their 'Prime Minister.'

Here, in the Chess Club the interest in the world at large was as vital and interesting as life had been a few years earlier. That was until Rory Asquith entered, and he got the second surprise. As he approached the Club, the doorman called to a table near by, "I think you should move a knight." People at each table in the corridor nearest the door all started talking about knights- and the atmosphere changed. It changed to such an extent that JID felt the room go colder, if not literally, then certainly emotionally. The people round the table all put on the familiar vague look. Players started making the kind of errors that beginners make. When Rory got near the table people greeted him without a hint of friendliness or any kind of emotion.

Rory moved to another table, but somebody said, "the knight is weaker but is still there." As he went round the corner behind the bar, a man who could see in that direction said something about horses, and the atmosphere resumed its former ease.

Mark and Nigel stopped their game - it had become a farce when Rory was around. JID found that Mark was a good person to talk to, and was soon chatting happily as if to an old friend. JID talked about his work and the way the atmosphere had been gradually changing. Mark said that he had heard similar reports from many people in all kinds of industries and commerce - it was something that all genuine people should resist in any way they can.

Mark continued his conversation about the state of society, and he seemed to talk more sense than all the people whom JID had met for a long time. JID asked why Mark had been on the 3Dvid. "You seem bright and unaffected, I thought you would realise. Still, I am sure there is hope for you yet!" laughed Mark.

"Mark is the Archbishop of Canterbury!" said Nigel. "Mark McCallow."

"But Joe King is the ABC! I saw him on the 3Dvid this afternoon. He has been the ABC for ten years and his first sermon hit the headlines. It was all about…" JID's voice trailed off, as he tried very hard to remember what had made that sermon so special even to his practical, fair, but irreligious mind. "It was about, erm…"

"I was instituted as Archbishop of Canterbury ten and a half years ago, having been the Bishop of Sheffield. At my induction service I spoke about the wrong direction of society and the ways that the country could avoid the worst effects of its current direction. I suggested that the current direction of society would lead to individuals having their individuality shredded by the effects of the existing selfish, godless, but financially rich society. Even the richness they worshipped would eventually be stripped away, but by then they would have lost any spirit to do anything about it. I said the world would become almost mechanical and people would become less valuable in their own and everyone else's eyes.

"Look around the country - and the rest of the world! I think I have been proved right."

JID was puzzled. He began to remember bits about the sermon, and how it had created so much debate at the time. Many sceptics recognised the truth of much of what he said, yet most people poured scorn on his answers. 'Archbishop of Canterbury proposes ancient answers to complex problems' was a typical headline.

The Archbishop had appeared on the TV that evening and argued that the answers had first been proposed about 2,000 years ago, yet were still the only ones that made sense. As a result of his sermon there had been a rise of about 12% in the number of people in Churches from the following Sunday. People wanted to find out more and many became regular attenders.

There had been silence in the conversation for about half a minute - not, this time, as a result of 'knights', but as JID tried to take in the implications of what was being said. Eventually he asked, "But what about Joe King? Where does he fit in? Isn't he the Archbishop?"

"A couple of years ago I was continuing my work as Archbishop. I was at home in Canterbury. I got up one morning and the 3Dvid news announced that the Archbishop of Canterbury, the ABC would be appearing live at 9.30am. I jumped up to look for the cameras and outside broadcast teams, but there was no sign of any action. I picked up the phone to contact my press secretary and the National News Agency, but the phone was dead, as was my computer. I jumped in the car to find that it, and all the family's cars, had had their tyres slashed.

"I went back into our quarters to find that the 'ABC' was just about to start speaking. Instead of watching a film of myself, I saw this fat ugly caricature grinning and spouting meaningless waffle about nothing in particular. He was scathingly humorous - very funny in some parts, but whoever he was and however he achieved it, everyone in the Government, the media and, in a few short minutes, 99% of the nation believed that he, Joe King, really was the Archbishop.

"A few minutes later the 'phone started to work and I took a call! The caller said that he was the secretary to Joe King and he wanted to make arrangements to take over my flat as my thinking and speaking had been declared unfit for general consumption. He said that if I was still in the flat in three hours time I would be taken out. He didn't actually define 'taken out', but I didn't wait to discover exactly what he meant.

"I originally came from Hesketh Bank, a village about ten miles from here, and had saved up enough to buy a house here, near enough to visit old friends. Churches became dangerous places! There was no danger to people's bodies, but they had mortal effects on minds and souls! Most clergy were shunted out of their livings, but some, like Joe King himself, became leaders of the new 'National Church.'

"What the Government failed to realise was that the Church can never be destroyed!" JID grinned - surely it *had* been destroyed. Mark saw his grin and continued - "Only the buildings are destroyed. The Church quickly metamorphosed." JID looked puzzled.

"That means it rapidly changed - like a caterpillar to a butterfly," said Mark.

"The real Church continues to meet, but in unlikely circumstances. In this area for instance the Hesketh

Bank Knitting Club, the Preston Stingers Rugby Union Club (they are the area champions), West Pennine Ramblers and the Mid-Lancashire Chess Club and their families are all Churches! There are many other Churches as well, but we exercise a certain self-discipline. We do not try to find out too much or have any paperwork or computer work about ourselves or others. That way the companies will not be able to track too many people down whenever they turn against us."

The mention of the Club being a Church made JID feel uneasy - he already knew what the companies could do to anyone they regarded as suspect. Now he seemed to be drawn to an illegal 'Church' organisation and was likely to land himself in much greater danger.

"One of our former clergy recently did a survey and found that about 20% of the population was a worshipping Christian- the highest since..."

Mark was interrupted by the doorman, who had not been concentrating but talking to a friend, suddenly singing at the top of his voice "Oh, what a night..." with particular emphasis on the word 'night'. Everyone went into their gormless mode.

JID glanced at the door, to see two people, not apparently together. One was a surly looking man of about forty, but the other was the most gorgeous-looking girl he had ever seen. He couldn't decide if he hoped she was the spy or not. Were they together or did they just arrive at the same time?

The atmosphere stayed overcast for about 20 minutes. The girl stood a few feet from JID, and the older man went from table to table, trying to talk about anything, but particularly about religion. When he came to JID's area, people just answered with grunts, and pretended to be more interested in the mockery of a chess game that was developing.

Eventually, after about half an hour, the man left. The doorman shouted "You've been very quiet, you must all have been hoarse." The doorman and a lot of the people (the congregation?) laughed and the easy, friendly conversation restarted. Mark stood up, read a few verses of the Bible and spoke about them, then said a prayer. Other people started to pray, and JID was surprised that they were praying FOR the company spies! Didn't these people recognise an enemy when they saw one!

JID thought that he would have felt uncomfortable when people were praying, but he felt an amazing calm. When the praying eventually stopped Mark spoke to JID, "I'd like you to meet my daughter, Ruth. Ruth, this is JID." The vision of beauty who had entered at the same time as the spy smiled and JID felt like he was melting. For a few sentences they were both nervous and could hardly speak, but soon they were chatting away. Chess was a common interest, but they seemed to share so much more and an attraction quickly grew.

At 10.30pm the people in the Club began to disperse so that they would beat the 11pm. curfew. JID and Ruth shook hands very formally. JID wanted to hug and kiss her, although with both fathers around it may have proved embarrassing. His father phoned for transport.

. . . . .

Early the next evening, before Nigel usually left for the Club, there was a knock on the door. Sarah answered, and then led Mark, Ruth and her mother, Jane, into the room. Mark always filled the space with his presence, and said that he was spending the evening visiting people in his congregation. Before long they were in prayer. This time JID felt more a part of the praying, although his mind tended to drift to Ruth quite often.

It was almost 7.30pm. and Nigel said that he had some confidential matters to discuss with Mark and Jane, so could JID and Ruth go to sort out drinks and biscuits. Their discussion would only take a few minutes.

JID and Ruth went to the kitchen and were soon laughing and joking. Ruth claimed to be the best chess player, and took a 3Dvid from her handbag. A chess board appeared and battle commenced. JID played well, but Ruth won the first two games. They continued for a while and forgot all about the refreshments. Suddenly there was a shout from Sarah, "Hadn't you better be getting Ruth home? It's a quarter to eleven!" Mark and Jane had left for another visit much earlier.

"Time really flies when you're having fun!" said Ruth.

"Yeah," mumbled JID, feeling suddenly self-conscious as he got ready to take her home.

They didn't use the transporters as it was a five minute walk to Ruth's flat, so JID walked with her. It was the first time for years that he had ventured out at night without transport. His happy conversation with Ruth continued. When they arrived, Ruth opened the front door and JID went to step in. Ruth pushed him away and said something about morality. JID realised that he was going to have to return to his parents' house, so he turned back.

He felt heartily sick. He had been with the girl of his dreams for a second special evening, but now he seemed to have blown all his chances. He had thought that she was as keen on him as he was on her, but had he imagined that his chances were better than they really were?

He arrived at home a few minutes later, avoided his parents and stormed up to his room.

. . . . .

JID had been in Preston for three weeks when he decided that he ought to go back and earn the money that would probably be paid anyway. He would stay for just one more night, but he would like to see Mark one more time to ask him if he had seen Ruth and try to find out if had completely blown his chances. He needn't have worried. Ruth arrived before her father and ran up to JID, who was in mid-chess game with another young man at the Club. She gave him a big smile and a kiss on the cheek.

"I think you're great!" she said.

JID didn't know what to make of her greeting and proceeded to try to find out, oblivious to his chess opponent who was an unfortunate witness to what was becoming a very intimate conversation. The opponent decided it would be best to slip away quietly.

JID told Ruth that it was difficult to understand her. All his friends would have been in bed together by now.

Ruth said, "But some things are even more important than sex."

JID was not sure what she would be likely to say next. Ruth certainly had some weird ideas.

"Faithful Christians wait for marriage!" she continued.

"But the Church, the companies and the Government have banned marriages, haven't they?" protested JID.

"It does not matter what they say. They are only trying to destroy people's lives in any way they can. I want real marriage, not just piling into bed with anyone."

JID felt offended to be described as 'anyone', but decided to quit while he was not too far behind. JID and Ruth set the board up and played against each other. Soon they were back in that wonderful world of new love. JID was convinced that she was the one (or to be more precise, he desperately *hoped* she was.) It is a pity that he had started so badly.

At the end of the evening JID walked her to her flat. He said that he would be going home the next day. He smiled at Ruth and asked if he could keep in contact by 3Dvid. "You'd better!" she said, and they parted with a passionate kiss.

It was 11.20pm. by the time JID arrived at his parents' house. He was so bowled over by Ruth that even the threat of the various company Order Brigades beating him up for breaking the curfew didn't occur to him. He walked into his parents' home as if he was walking on air.

He was leaving for home the next afternoon. He got up early and reflected on the previous days, hopeful yet still confused about Ruth. He had few people he could talk to about it. Everyone at work - and most of the other people he was likely to meet were completely bamboozled by the companies' mindbending, so they would either ignore him or, if they had any brain left, they would realise that he had been mixing with 'undesirable' people and his life could be in danger.

The only people he could think of were his own parents or Ruth's. Although he had not had a very deep conversation with them for years, he decided on his own parents. When his father appeared for his breakfast JID decided to ask him about Ruth.

"If I was your age and hadn't met your mother she would be top of my list!" his father enthused. "Where else could you find someone with a mind of her own yet such a great sense of loyalty. She is witty. She is intelligent. She has the best body I have seen for decades - and she is good at chess!"

JID was taken aback by his father's directness. It seems he had asked the right person. "But…" JID didn't quite know how to ask the next one. "But marriage is banned. Everyone just does it without marriage- even without thinking. We had a great time together. Laughing, joking, playing, even cuddling yet she wouldn't let me! She complained when I tried to get into the house. Surely she must be a lesbian or something. Whatever it is, it seems to be affecting her whole life!"

"You're right, it is affecting her whole life. But I don't think she's lesbian." His father explained. "She holds to traditional values. For the last fifteen years the media have been banned from even considering that there may be traditional values! It's all part of the conspiracy to turn people from what is right."

"So there is no future for me with her!" JID complained. "I'm just ordinary. You're no archbishop and I'm no son-in-law of one! She is talking perfection here. She must be the only perfect person in the country under the age of 80 to think that way! I could never fit in to that ideal.

"You have got it all wrong!" said his father. "I don't play chess just because I enjoy it. I'd rather sit at home and watch the 3Dvid. I go to the chess club because that is my church! I WANT to be there! I want to worship God because that is the only reality. It is the best reality. It is the only way a person can shake himself clear of the humdrumness that the world has descended into. If you want what is best you have to be prepared to make sacrifices! God made sacrifices for us so I want to please Him!

JID was beginning to warm to his father's position, yet he could not figure out why. He also had another question to ask. "How come you have gone religious? You never were when I was growing up. You have completely changed. You've been caught! Hook, line and sinker!"

"You're right!" Nigel nodded. "I think God planned it all. I kept meeting people, all kinds of people who seemed to know something special that I had missed. Eventually it clicked - they are all Christians. I started to go to a Church but since the Church fell I have been going to the Chess Club. It all makes sense."

Nigel paused for a moment, then continued, "You have a choice to make. Do you want to become as dozy as the rest of the world - or do you want something much better? Real Christianity is better than the best experienceometry gadget."

JID wanted to leave for the transport home soon, so he had to go to pack. He had a much better relationship with his father than previously, but he was convinced that you could resist the companies without going to the religious extreme.

It occurred to him that Nigel was desperately hoping that he would get together with Ruth, but, even after all their talking, Nigel hadn't given him any clue about how to go about it. Surely a girl like this one would need a strategy beyond his own ideas. She had obviously been influenced by her father, but, without knowing more about their philosophy, JID was on his own.

On the way home JID snoozed, and dreamt about Ruth. She would be just the right one for him, yet how could he ever succeed with her? Would he need to become a religious nutter, or her become a friendly atheist. Or was there some middle ground where they could meet?

When he was in the privacy of home he sent her a 3Dvid. He decided to be straightforward with her and see where that got him. "I… I think I love you. I'm desperately in love. You are the best girl I have ever met. You are beautiful in every way. And you have something special that few people have." He decided that this 3Dvid note was too corny for words and slammed his hand down on the delete key. He missed and sent the note to Ruth.

Five minutes later she replied with a Vidnote of her own. "That's the nicest thing anyone has ever said to me. I enjoyed being with you and cannot wait for the next time you are in Preston. I think I like you."

JID was still confused. Did she love him? Did she like him? And what does she think the difference is?

They continued to talk on 3D Vid in the days ahead, and JID still had her in his sights!

He went back to work the next day, enlivened by Ruth, his and her families, and the other friends he had made in Preston. They seemed more alive than anyone else he had seen for ages.

When he got to work he hanged his coat up and shouted, "Hello, everyone. I have had a fantastic time." Most didn't respond, but one or two looked up and said, "Hello", before returning their mouths and their minds to their cups of coffee.

# Chapter 4. April.
# The State of the World...

"Hello, here is the news for the 3rd of April from the Information Centre of European Governments," crooned the 3Dvid newsman. He wore a smart, bright yellow suit with red collars, over his green shirt and grey tie. "In a few moments I, Phantom Smith will be bringing you the latest from our nations and the world."

JID had had the 3Dvid on in the background, but when he heard the news announced he decided to pour a Timbros during the adverts that always followed the initial announcement. The 3Dvid image changed to show the unmistakable face of Malc Mitchum, and JID heard the applause coming from the screen and the next house. He tried to turn the sound lower before leaving the room but was unable to. 'Shoddy rubbish', he thought to himself - the 3Dvid receiver was malfunctioning even though he had bought it new just 6 months ago. He then had another thought - was it poor equipment, or was it another way the companies were getting a closer grip on the life of the country - making sure you heard the adverts? He shuddered at the thought and went into the kitchen, where he could hear the screen next door, but, mercifully, it sounded much quieter.

He boiled the kettle and made his tea. He sent a 3Dvid to Ruth. He went to the kitchen and got some biscuits out. He went back to the 3Dvid room, thinking that it was time for the adverts to finish. He was wrong! A Shopafrolic advert started as he entered. Uniformed Shopafrolic operatives, looking very like the ones who had kidnapped him from the conference, were smiling and telling the world that their job was to make the customers' lives easier, happier and more *real!* JID cringed at the sight of them. They continued to cajole the minds of the mindless with tall tales about how they could make life more interesting / eventful / calm / thrilling / relaxing / exciting and so on. All you needed was various devices which they could only buy from Shopafrolic. JID realised that several of the promised emotions were in fact opposed to each other, but most of the listening public would buy the tale anyway. Could they only buy these devices from Shopafrolic? JID had seen them for sale in the local Livershop just days earlier.

JID waited patiently for the news, trying very hard not to be too influenced by the horror that he felt every time he saw any adverts, which were all for the megacompanies and their products. Eventually the screens cut to the newsreader. Phantom Smith in 3d appeared uncomfortably close to JID, who instinctively moved his chair a metre back.

"Hello, and now for the news, and we start with a scoop! The national transport network, NWET, continues to improve." JID nodded. It was the only part of life that had improved in the last few years. "Livershop and Megatrade have cooperated to make it easy to get around our land. Formerly air travel was costly and dangerous. Most people are amazed at the primitiveness of the cars, wagons and trains that were part of our lives until recently. Our Government and companies have combined to make life easier in transport as in every part of life. Gravity-reversal technology has given us a transport system that we would have thought was sheer science fiction until recently. Combining the old Satellite Navigation techniques into these transporters, our wonderful machines take you quickly and safely to where you want to go, cutting costs as we use only a fraction of the fuel, and do not have to maintain roads or railways!

JID knew that he had heard this 'Scoop' four times in the previous month, but was still fascinated by the achievement of the transport system. However, he had also realised that when an old, encouraging report was rehashed, there was usually bad news to come. He wondered if the companies were hoping that people would get bored and turn off, literally, or at least mentally, before they got to a bad bit.

"Do you remember the old days of airports, stations and bus stations?" Phantom continued, "How many of us have lost our tickets and our tempers there. How many hours have we had to wait as connections were missed or services temporarily suspended? What can be better than calling for transport from home and the transporter coming to your door? Instead of going to an airport the size of a medium sized town you are whisked quickly and safely from your door or from one of the 78,000 minor transporter stations to one of the 3,500 major stations, and step from your personal carriage straight on to the main carriage and be at your destination in a very short time. Times from any part of NWE (even the most remote part) to Liverpool are all less than 35 minutes, and the speed is just as good if you are not going to and from major centres.

JID noticed a bit of reality-creep! It actually took 40 minutes to get from Northampton to Liverpool, but it was still much faster than any previous method.

"Most of us are fascinated having these silent" (a small exaggeration!) "machines zooming just above our roofs, but all generations have their reactionary groups that try to prevent progress. Even the NWE Transport Lobby, that excellent but misguided group of Luddites, has decided that it really is a good idea. Their former president, Jules Barnet is ready to give us an interview.

JID was surprised to note that this part of the broadcast was being shown for the first time. Jules Barnet was 1.95 metres tall. He had been a regular commentator on national life in recent years, and was instantly recognisable to most people. His kindly manner and gracious speaking, combined with his quick mind and sometimes outspoken views made him a popular figure on 'Questions for Now' and other talk shows. (What had happened to these shows in recent years?) JID was glad to be able to hear Jules Barnet again as he had brightened up many of the old TV Programme. However, when Jules appeared on the screen JID was horrified at what he saw. Jules, who was now in his early forties, looked like an 80 year old. He had bruises on his face and was walking with a stoop.

"I was sorry to hear about your accident," said an unseen female reporter. JID walked around the image of Jules Barnet and could see swellings on his cheeks and eyebrows, clearly the result of several blows.

"Yes, I fell off my seat when I got sleepy. It's good to know that free speech is alive and well!" said Jules, and JID could tell that that comment was ironic. JID was behind Jules at the time and saw what few would see and nobody was supposed to see. A videoprompt in front of Jules flashed up the words "Stick to the script or you will suffer the consequences."

Jules had proved many times that he was both honest and brave. He did stick to the script, but he pointed to the words on the videoprompt as he spoke. Many of the audience in their homes ran to the back of Jules and caught a glimpse of the videoprompt, before the presenters realised their mistake and took the prompt from the transmission.

Pointing to the words, Jules said "I realise that my opposition to the NWET was mistaken and misplaced. What better way for the people to travel. Following our magnificent, wise leaders in Government and commerce is the way forward for today and for all time.

Jules saw that the presenters had relaxed and were having their own way, and said "They haven't told you the real consequences of NWET! They don't want anyone to know that, in a combination of various conditions, the...

The screen went blank, and a disembodied voice said "We seem to have lost our transmission. Perhaps we will go back to Jules Barnet later. We will continue with other parts of our broadcast."

The screen went back to the part of the broadcast that JID had heard before. The cameras were above the Liver Bird statues on the Livershop Building near the river in Liverpool. The skies were full of transporters and considerably darker as a result. Local transporters were the ones at the lower level and long range transporters above them. They flew at hundreds of miles an hour, missing each other and taller buildings by centimetres. It was all controlled by satnavs and computers, and worked incredibly well. A scientist in a white coat was seen sitting on top of a Liver Bird, looking very uncomfortable! He started to describe the achievement of technology that had made the new system possible, in a voice specially designed to bore the mind and make it look as if he knew what he was talking about. He didn't, of course! He was just an actor spouting lines given to him. It had nothing to do with the real technology involved, but was put there to mislead anyone who may attempt to imitate it or pass information to Gaucho Gonzales or other associated guerrilla groups. As in so many other ventures, Gonzales's technical teams were one step ahead. They knew about the product even before it was produced and it was their people who had alerted Jules Barnet of the potential dangers.

After a couple of minutes the 3Dvid watcher found himself alongside Jules Barnet once again. Jules said, "I am sorry about my earlier broadcast. I want you to know that the transport system is genuine."

He wiped his brow with the back of his right hand and had clearly crossed his first two fingers. NWET never has and never will cause anybody any problems."

After days of violent conditioning by the TV company's thugs and psychologists, they did not think that Jules Barnet had any fight left in him, but they were dealing with the wrong man! His bravery had meant that there was controversy in the first main item. However, they then went on to the very mundane items, all suitably filmed beforehand to avoid any possible intrusion into the megacompanies' agenda.

Phantom Smith continued, "Now for the sports news. All the top teams have been playing today, and it's really happening at the top of the Superleague. Tranmere Rovers are in second place after a creditable 2-2 draw at Old Trafford. The Manchester team are still third although Liverpool won once again, 3-1 at home to Leeds, and are now just one point behind them. Now for scenes of the action..."

The audience were shown the 3Dvids of the best moments of the matches. JID liked to be on the pitch for the matches on 3Dvid, although there were many times when he (like all other close-up 3Dvid watchers) took a kick at the ball and his foot went right through it! The commentator enthused that it was now getting closer at the top. The goals from seven matches followed. JID was glad to see that Northampton won an exciting match away to Stockport County by 5-3, to overtake them and move into twelfth place. JID wondered why the commentator had not mentioned Merziblu, the team that he thought was now top of the Superleague. Was this another case of organised reality-creep? Had they been guilty of 'unacceptable' thinking to the megacompanies? Had they for some reason found themselves on the Government or companies' blacklist?

The broadcast continued, "We now have news of the religious scene in North America, Ian Dunnet has been overwhelmingly voted as the leader of the United Evangelical Church of the USA following the arrest of 28 former leaders of what had been a corrupt movement which claimed to have contact with what they called the Holy Spirit. The charges ranged from corrupt use of their office, claiming their way was exclusive, making extreme claims about pseudo-historical figures such as Jesus of Nazareth as well as lesser crimes such as extortion and robbery.

We now move to Washington DC, where our reporter, Jim Carna is ready to speak to us. What can you tell us, Jim?

The viewer was instantly transported to a site near the White House, where Jim Carna was looking towards the viewer, but was glancing frequently to his left to see if there was any more news.

"We may be able to tell you more soon. This case went straight to the Supreme Court and we are expecting a verdict at any time. As soon as we get a verdict we will let you know, but for now let's go to the courtroom. We do suggest that people of a nervous disposition shut their eyes for the next few minutes

The view was replaced by the courtroom, with a large cage holding the 28 former leaders. The prisoners seemed to be happy despite their predicament. All had hands tied behind their backs. One was seen to be whispering to another who listened, smiled and then nodded. The first man started to spit on the clothing of the second, and then rub his face in the spittle. Make-up came off to show bruises. Others started to do the same.

Where the 3Dvid cameras had been showing the whole courtroom, they suddenly turned to just show the judge. The 3Dvid producers of the American Programme, as twisted as the ones in NWE, were using similar techniques to attempt to blot out any image that would give a 'wrong' impression. The judge stood to speak to the court. He glared towards the cage and said, "What have you miserable worms got to say for yourselves."

One counted "1-2-3" and the whole lot sang,

> "Despite the hatred and rage
> > of many sinners and the sage
> > Jesus died to set me free!
> (The judge yelled "Silence!")
> > He suffered for all who will follow Him,
> > And that's enough for me!"

The screen was suddenly silenced again, although it was not clear whether the offending Christians shut up as directed or if the sound was turned off by the 3Dvid station. An unseen reporter apologised for the accidental vile intrusion of illegal religious rhetoric. The judge had the courtroom cleared of these 'offenders' and the trial continued as if nothing had happened! Several people came forward to say how members of their families had been influenced by people like these. Their children, brothers and sisters had started to smile a lot of the time and some had changed jobs because they thought that the employers ("who are all genuine, God-fearing entrepreneurs") were misleading customers. "Revolutionaries like these cannot be tolerated," claimed one member of the public.

The judge asked if there was anyone who was representing the defendants. As the defendants had had their resources confiscated and their accounts frozen they could not pay the huge price of a firm of lawyers. A man in his early twenties, the son of one of the defendants stood up and asked to address the court. The judge gave him a sneering glance and said, "OK, but make it quick."

"My name is Maurice Ruggers. I have no formal qualifications, yet, as I am in my final year of a law degree at Harvard I have some understanding of the legal system. So far this trial has produced no genuine evidence against any of these so-called offenders. I will show that several Articles of the US Constitution have been...

The 3Dvid broadcast of the court ceased abruptly. (Yet another case of censorship for the benefit of the megacompanies, political rulers, or both - thought JID). Phantom Smith continued,

"The President of the USA gave a statement.

Viewers found themselves in the Oval Office of the White House, listening to the President. "We will continue to do all in our power to ensure that the religious field is open to all genuine people. The United Evangelical Church of the USA, or UECUSA, will now be able to take its place among the growing number of

Churches that are ready to lose their own identity to join with groups such as the New Anglican Church in NEW, led by Joe King. The old religion of specifics is being confined to the history books and we will soon be able to formally join Worldfaith! Joe King and Pope Shambolic will be appearing on talk shows across America soon with their humorous, but carefully thought out presentation of their beliefs. Most people in this great nation of ours already hold these beliefs and so the nation need no longer exclude open discussion of religion from the public square. In due course it may become illegal for people to oppose these views in the interest of public safety. I salute the new leaders of UECUSA who will lead us all forward in this great emotional and intellectual quest for truth and freedom.

Phantom Smith appeared on the screens again. "Yes", he said in a much louder voice than usual - like a sports commentator when a goal is scored, "Freedom is becoming possible even in the USA. The old religion is being replaced by the real thing!

The scene switched once more. The viewer was in a field with horses about ten metres away. One of the horses left the group and it became apparent that it was actually two people in a horse suit - an almost lifelike Pantomime horse! The front part of the horse took its head off to reveal Joe King. "Hello! It's really me, the ABC", he giggled. "Even the evangelicals are now on board with the new, true faith," he claimed.

Guess who is following close behind me! It's none other than..." He pointed behind himself.

The back end of the horse was pulled over the head of the new head of UECUSA, Ian Dunnet. "It's me, I. Dunnet, all on my own! (with the cooperation of the Archbishop here)" he called. "In our country we have had to work carefully to see the way forward. We have had stronger religious organisations here than in many parts of the world so we have had to strive harder to find the best way to deal with extremism. Now that UECUSA has been cleansed of the moral laxity in its leaders it will become the rallying point of true faith in this mighty nation. People of other denominations and faiths will be welcomed into it, and we will put on trial any who make extreme claims for any kind of the old divisive religious systems. A new unity and freedom will follow!

The screen changed and the viewer was led between several different scenarios. In each one the people were relaxed and laughing. In JID's experience the only place where this had happened in the last decade was the Chess Club in Preston. "People in NWE, your nation and mine, can be happier than ever!" said an unseen reporter. "The freedom of the nation and of the world is becoming real to all of us."

JID wondered where these scenes were filmed, as he walked among the people being featured. They didn't show the tired boredom of the people with whom he worked. They didn't show the sarcastic smugness of the leaders of the New Anglican Church or any of its associates. They didn't show the false smiles of Kenneth Kippam. The reporter continued, "These are people who realise and accept that the companies and Worldfaith are the way to true happiness. Old uncertainties are now replaced. We asked some of the people involved the reason for their happiness.

Various scenes of happy people followed, with voices in the background. The voices were not those of the happy people on the various changing screens.

"I am happy with my lot because I get a contentment in the safety of the companies," said the first one. Others followed, spouting the same kind of sentiments that JID had heard at the Liverpool conference.

JID continued to see the screens of happy people, and then to his surprise JID found himself in familiar territory - the Chess Club in Preston! Somehow the authorities had got a 3Dvid camera into the Club without being spotted by the doorman. His father, Mark McCallow and several of his friends from Preston were playing chess and laughing and joking. A female voice with a Welsh accent, that JID had not heard in Preston said, "In our Chess Club we enjoy the finer things in life because we have the new religion and appreciate the friendliness of the companies.

"Isn't this wonderful," sang Joe King. "And now ABC joins USA! No. It is the other way around! Whatever... we are all one in our thinking and our actions. No need to concern ourselves with trivological the-ality, er, theological triviality." He paused while he laughed at his own spoonerism. "Everything is beautiful," he declared before starting to sing the Ray Steven's song from the previous century and he then said, "Weren't the Beatles a magnificent group!"

JID realised that the people who were being shown on the screen were really happy - but not because of their submissive attitude to the spurious authorities! Not one of them was actually seen speaking to the cameras!

Phantom Smith reappeared in front of JID, and he looked genuinely worried for the first time ever on TV. "We have some grave news from Western Asia. Our spy satellites have detected movement of forces travelling southwards on a broad front between the Caspian Sea and the Black Sea. Israel stated that they insist the convoy stops before they reach Turkey or Syria. Their President said, "We regard this movement as a threat and will respond vigorously to any threat to our sovereignty."

Viewers saw a satellite 3Dvid of the world, which zoomed in to show a huge army of tanks and transporters.

"China has said that they do not know the purpose of the invasion, but that in the interest of their own security, they would be sending forces to the region. And now a word from our sponsors…

The screens went into the normal round of adverts for megacompanies. JID went to the kitchen and prepared a snack. He left longer than ever for the adverts, still to return before they finished. Recently he had timed them and found that the adverts took up about 40% of the total time whichever channel you watched.

Smith reappeared. "Do not let that last announcement spoil your day. I am sure it is not as bad as it seems" he said, with a smile that somehow did not seem genuine. "Now for some other international news. We have a report about the situation in many parts of Africa. Our man in Guineberia is Albert Switstein. Albert, what can you tell us about the lifestyle there?

The scene moved to a clearing in the tropical rainforest with a few mud huts in the background. JID's room began to smell of urine and mangroves. (The most recent 3Dvids had an aroma attachment). "In many places throughout Africa, life continues in much the same way that it has for millennia! People in this village, for example, carry out subsistence farming throughout the year. Some younger family members go to school, but, in the holidays, they join their relations in their late teens and twenties in the rice swamps. Nearer home are their fields of ginger, an occasional pineapple plant, lots of luscious fruit from the trees and, if the family is well off, they may own a goat. Is this the kind of life for them for all time? We asked some for their opinions"

The reporter talked to some of the locals asking their impressions of their life. Most of them talked of their want for more food and civilisation. One talked about her Christian faith, and the voice of Switstein said that it was not surprising that uncivilised people should have uncivilised beliefs. The comments of the people moved from general topics to them expressing their craving for western goods and prosperity.

"Where the missionaries failed, Livershop has succeeded. From villages, to megacities in this great continent, new Livershop branches have opened with the express aim of helping these desperately poor people into the 21$^{st}$ century! We do not care about their background or their history, we are only concerned about their future."

JID wondered how the news itself had become an advert. "Africa is really advancing at last! In keeping with all civilised initiatives," continued Switstein, "it is a strictly secular venture. Old religions such as Christianity and Hinduism need have no further hold on the populations of people such as these!"

'Since when have people in Africa been Hindu?' thought JID.

"It is reported that some communities are holding on to their former superstitions, like Christianity, so naturally they are not yet ready to accept the largesse of our company. We and the Government of Guineberia will deal with these rebels on two fronts to prevent them from peddling their harmful ideologies, which try to stop the benevolent work of our..."

He hesitated and corrected himself, "of the company involved. We... they will not invest in any development in those communities and their banks will, rightly, freeze any of their assets that they hold. In extreme cases of groups who still hold out against the companies, it will be clear that they are nothing more than rebellious reactionary revolutionaries and will be dealt with as such.

"There are reports that some religious groupings have left their villages and gone to live in the dense rainforest where it is difficult for land forces to track them down. A reasonable cooling off period will be given, when they will be able to retract and return to their old villages with the new conditions. After that they will be tracked by satellites and hunted down by air. It is a sad situation, but the only way that the genuine members of the population will be able to be kept safe. There are so many promising signs, and soon Africa will be able to fully enjoy the benefits of an economy like the one enjoyed by so many in Europe and North America."

JID found himself facing Phantom Smith, who still had a smile that seemed to be covering up a worried expression. The scene switched to today's interviews with 'the average man in the street.' As they were genuine interviews, the interviewees wore one of the usual three expressions.

"Why should I be worried in a land of benevolent companies?" said one, with a bland expression that showed no emotion whatsoever.

"The Government will protect us," said another, with a smile that was obviously false.

"We have to put our faith in the ABC and the recent religion," said another, looking downright sad.

"These people truly are genuine," said Phantom Smith. "Their joy is real, unlike the forced emotions of North Korea and other places that resisted the persuasion of the companies' philosophy until very recently. In places like that people were unable to make sensible decisions. They were forced to conform by fair means or foul. They were unable to vote or challenge the powerful ones. They could not even think for themselves! How, different it is in our land of freedom and liberty. NWE is the true home of freedom and justice.

'Oh, really?' thought JID.

# Chapter 5. May.
# The Joy and the Pain...

JID had been 3Dviding Ruth for the last 30 minutes and the conversation continued, partly live and partly edited before the messages were sent. He could see that the land was slipping into economic and social ruin so he said, "I think that this nation stinks!"

Then he stopped to think. Perhaps he had better not send that on his 3Dvid line. Ruth would have no problem with it - she would almost certainly agree and even if she didn't, she would not cause a problem over it. He wasn't worried about her, but about the companies. Ever since the Liverpool event he had realised that they seemed to know every time a person sneezed. If he sent a 3Dvid, someone, somewhere would be likely to read it and pass the information on to the companies. It then occurred to him that, even though he had not transmitted the message, it may have already been viewed by their staff. However, he cancelled that statement and thought how he could respond honestly and say what he meant, but without offending the hierarchy.

He missed Ruth. He would have been to see her before then but the ever reliable transport links were no longer so reliable. He had listened to the official news bulletins regularly, thinking that what amounted to a complete shutdown of the nation's transport deserved some sort of acknowledgement, but his searches proved fruitless.

He sent a different message to Ruth. "We have to stay strong and move on, even if there are difficulties sometimes."

Ruth was clearly in tune with what was on JID's mind, and she was a lot less worried (or maybe a lot more naïve) than JID. She told her 3Dvid to transmit live instead of on consideration-mode. "There are lots of times when I find Northwesteurope difficult to cope with!" she said "And I don't care who knows that I said it! When you look around people are all either making a fortune out of 'the system' or seem to be too dozy to care. It cannot carry on indefinitely! Simple laws of economics make it impossible." (Now JID was overwhelmed by Ruth's understanding of events as she continued in depth about economic, social and political theory and practice. His mind wandered as her analysis went way above his head and he started to think about the wonderful, clever woman he was friendly with and her beautiful body. Would she, could she, ever be his?)

"Well, what do you think?" said Ruth.

JID was startled. Ruth was calling him out of his daydreams and back to the real world. He clicked back to live transmission. "Er... Er... What do I think about what?" he said, feeling very embarrassed.

"About what I have been saying."

JID did some mental fumbling and said "I agree. I think you fully understand the situation."

"But I asked your detailed opinion about my last argument."

JID then admitted that he had been miles away. Ruth knew that and started to laugh. She asked what he had been thinking about, and JID decided to be honest. "I am in love with a beautiful woman and I'd like to be in bed with her and spend my life with her. I'm talking about you! I am head over heels in love with you. I like your body and your mind. Where else can I find a woman who is neither stupid nor shallow. You don't try to look sexy but you can't help it! You think deeply about things and you are concerned about other people and the world around you. We need to get together! How about it? Next time I can get to Preston!"

"You're very special to me and you have been since we first met. I have been praying about it and expected you to ask!"

"Never mind praying. What's your answer, I can't wait for ever!" JID interrupted, then realised that would not be the most reliable way to win his religious woman. "I'm sorry, I must remain calm, but it is so important to me. I love you very much and your answer means so much to me - I think that it will make or break my life."

"I love you," she said. JID's mind went into overdrive thinking what this meant for him. It was the first time she had admitted loving him, then she added "but the time is not right."

JID certainly seemed to have created a chance for himself. He took a lot of comfort from the conversation. They stayed talking, live, for the next couple of hours, but generally on comparatively trivial issues. They had some games of chess, and JID actually won one for the first time - although he wondered if she had let him win to reassure him! They talked about their homes and their families and cabbages and kings. When they said goodnight Ruth squeezed his virtual hand and kissed his virtual face. It was as near to the real thing as he ever got, but not surprisingly JID wanted more.

When they stopped talking and settled for the night JID couldn't get to sleep. He was excited by Ruth's half-promise but was worried about what she had said and possible consequences if the companies found out about some of her comments. Would she be subjected to some horrendous experience like the one JID suffered in Liverpool? Had he inadvertently said something to which the companies would take exception? Would he have to face another ordeal like he suffered in

Liverpool, a second phase of humiliation? What would that involve? Could he survive?

His mind was in a spin. His thoughts went from bliss at what might be, to uncertainty about where he really stood with Ruth, to fear of the companies, all within a few seconds - and then back to the start. After what seemed like days, he realised that he wasn't going to get any sleep in the near future so he decided to direct his mind elsewhere and started to think about the population of Northwesteurope. What was it that made people click? Who was where the companies wanted them to be? Was anyone resisting, and how effectively? Was there, perhaps, any organised resistance movement? Might he be able to join it? Were the companies even trying to use the resistance in some diabolical fashion? And what about the revolutionary rebels who had taken over part of Heathrow? Where did JID himself stand in all of this? And Ruth? And their families? And the people in Preston Chess Club? And the new clergy who were strongly and violently against the quaint religious traditionalism of Ruth's father?

JID thought about the revolutionaries. Were they the ones who were correct? It was very difficult to know. Most thinking people (the few that were left) realised that the official news Programme must be well wide of the mark. If the rebels were against the Government but had been firmly defeated, how could they put banners all over the outside walls of a former terminal building in the old Heathrow Airport? Why did the

Government conveniently fail to mention it in their publicity about the airport? JID thought about his own chess abilities, and Ruth's. This kind of skill would surely be useful to the revolutionaries, or to the Government or the companies, or whoever the real goodies were. Should they join one of the groups to overthrow the others? He imagined himself becoming the hero of possible battle scenes, giving revolutionary forces the ideas and intelligence to overcome the existing regime, with the beautiful Ruth at his side. Perhaps they would occasionally join in with weapons like the fictitious James Bond did in 2d films in previous decades. But if the revolutionaries were really part of the regime he would be executed or worse before he would be able to achieve anything. How could he find out the truth about the revolutionaries' aims- and would Ruth like the idea of armed resistance anyway? He decided that this could never be the best way. He grinned at how brave he was in his dreams and wondered if he could ever be as brave as that in real life. In the following months he would find out.

JID thought about Government soldiers. If rumours were true they had been so passive, and their leadership so bad that when the revolutionaries invaded they didn't even put up an effective fight. What caused their stupor? Would he be able to become an apparently reformed character and gain a high rank in the army? Then he would be able to reverse the drugs, psychological tricks or whatever else it was that had blown the minds of the soldiers under him. They could take over the army with ease and start to work on the rest of society. At some future date they may be able to restore the nation to something like what it had been before the changes of the last decade or two. Again he decided it would not work - for the same reasons.

JID thought about the company security men. They were being asked to carry out tasks that were, at best, mean and, at worst, evil - but they had a secure job and a reliable take home pay. They knew that as long as their company existed they would be OK. There was no guarantee that the companies would last for ever, but it seemed the safest bet so far. Again he would have the problem of convincing some very unsavoury characters that he was now on their side, but he was resourceful enough to be able to carry it off. He then thought of his own integrity and the certainty that any association with the companies would do no good to his chances with Ruth - and so he continued his thinking in a different direction.

Other people who seemed to enjoy their work were sports stars. He had fondly imagined that one day he would become 'JID Davies of Northampton and Northwesteurope.' Many of his school friends had had similar dreams. Most, like JID, had never been able to get above local teams playing on local parks. There was one exception. Neil Young had turned into a top player. His flame coloured hair had earned him the nickname 'Red' and that name had stuck. Red played for one of the teams in the capital, Merziblu, which was currently top of the Superleague. Red was a hard midfielder, 1.92

metres tall. For a midfielder he scored a lot of goals, mainly by launching his considerable frame in the right direction and heading the ball at bullet speed to the goal. JID was surprised at Red's discipline on the pitch. At school he could stamp out the best of the opponent's attacks and often score a goal in the first ten minutes. However, he was not always picked for the team! Often when he stamped out an attack he did it by stamping on the opponent! He rarely played more than 20 minutes before being sent off for a foul tempered tirade or often for what was euphemistically called a professional foul, even in the very amateur scene of school matches. Some of the best players in other schools ended up in hospital after mixing with Red. The disciplinarian teacher who picked the team easily lost patience with him and dropped him, before eventually giving him a lecture about team discipline two weeks later and giving him yet another 'last chance'.

When he thought about Red, JID was always amazed by the change in his character now that he was in top football. The school's hard man now played just as hard, but for the second year in a row he had won the midfielders fair play award. He had never been sent off while playing for Northampton earlier in his career, for Merziblu or for NWE. In five years he had been booked just four times, and two of those were officially cancelled when the football authorities reviewed 3Dvid evidence.

Red must have been, like all the top footballers in Northwesteurope, a multibillionaire. He probably would have no interest in a person from his school who had played (badly) in the same team, but hadn't generally been in the same social group. And that was all eight or nine years earlier. Still, JID thought that it would be good to get in touch with Red. Red would have an insight into another side of life in the Northwesteurope, and perhaps help JID in trying to work out just how the country was working and what he should do about it. Footballers were among the few people who were alert to themselves and the world, but had not yet been drawn into the general stupor all around them.

JID got out of bed, and went to the Merziblu website. He spoke a few instructions and went to 'Talk to a player'. At the top of the page it said in prominent letters

> *The Merziblu Stars are very busy people!*
> *You are allowed one application*
> *to speak to a player each season*
> *and if your request is turned down*
> *you will have to be content*
> *with listening to players' 3Dblogs.*

He scrolled down and clicked on Red Young. A voice said, "Your 3dblog will be sent to Red Young. He will reply if he sees your communication and is able to respond. If he does not have time he apologises and sends his best wishes. Your blog time will start at the tone."

JID heard the bleep and started to talk, trying to look cool and on top of life. "Hi, Red. You probably don't remember me. I played in the Northampton Academy team with you. I hope that you will be able to contact me as I appreciate the way you have become an international great in football. You play a clean game, yet always achieve great things. I still have an ordinary job in Northampton and am trying to better myself. I have recently fallen for a girl called Ruth McCallow and I play chess…"

JID was really getting into his stride, but the computer declared, "You have had enough time to do a simple initial message. Our star may call you back if he is able. This website is registered with the NWE Superleague and is protected by all the appropriate legal bodies. If you or…"

The computer droned on with the usual messages. It must have been good in the old days when all that was in text on the screen and you didn't have to listen to it all! But JID felt that he had made a fool of himself. He must look like a real no-hoper to the next captain of NWE. He was glad that he was a couple of hundred kilometres from Liverpool and the potential embarrassment of ever accidentally meeting Red.

. . . . .

The next Saturday, Merziblu were due to play at Northampton and early on Friday evening JID's doorbell rang. His eyes nearly popped out as he went to the door to be confronted by the giant figure of Red Young himself! He went into an uncharacteristically nervous mode and splurted, "I... I'm sorry !... That 3Dvid message was..."

Red grinned and said, "Calm down! Don't worry! I come in peace!"

JID gathered his thoughts and invited Red into his flat. "It's great to see you!" was Red's opening gambit. "You are a man I respect!"

JID wondered what Red was going on about. "What did I do or say at school to make you think that?"

"Nothing to do with school! I have to admit that I hardly remember you at school - I'm very sorry. We are both friendly with the same beautiful woman - Ruth McCallow!" JID immediately looked terrified. Surely he hadn't been trying to poach the property of the giant sitting across the room from him, who had made most of the school thugs look like dormice.

"I do like her, but I'm not trying to take her from you," said JID to protect his freedom yet feeling sick that he had not had the guts to even admit his interest.

"Don't be daft" said Red. (The last time he had heard Red say that was after JID had miskicked a shot in stoppage time and the opponents took advantage, scored and won by one goal!)

"I don't love her like you do!" continued Red, "She is a close friend of my wife, Kit. Ruth is madly, head over heels in love with you! Surely you realise that!"

JID noted that Red had used the word 'Wife'! He thought that the word had almost disappeared from the NWE language, only to be used by people like Ruth and her father.

"After we played Preston in the Cup we both dropped in to see her and she told us all about you. When I got your email I couldn't resist finding out where you lived and taking the opportunity to drop in. She was so intense about her feelings towards you, Sunshine, that we began to think that the sun shone out of... out of you!"

'Sunshine' was another word that Red had used scathingly in the past, but now like the rest of his conversation and action it seemed to take on a special friendly tone.

JID felt slightly embarrassed at the way the conversation was going so he changed the subject. He didn't want to declare his love for Ruth too openly in case she would just keep on putting him off. "There has been a great change in you, Red" said JID. "Playing on your side was embarrassing for anyone who made a mistake, and playing against you was dangerous."

JID paused a moment, worried that he may rouse the fury of the beast of yesteryear, but when he saw that Red was happily grinning he continued. "Merziblu have been the 'Fair Play' kings for three years and you are the fairest midfielder. How do you keep your cool now? If someone at school had tackled you like the one you suffered against Liverpool you would have cracked his skull. You smiled at the Liverpool player and the lip-reading computer, Lipcom, reckoned you said something like 'Please do not do that again to me or anyone else! It's quite painful,' before they carried you off and you couldn't play for six weeks. If someone had told me that Red Young would do that when we were at school I would have said they were mad!

Red didn't bring the subject back to Ruth, but went with JID's topic. "I'm a changed man!" he said.

"I can see that," said JID. "But why?"

"What are the people like at the Chess Club?"

JID couldn't see the relevance of the change of subject. Chess opponents never kick and rarely swore! However, JID went with the subject. The memory of Joe Kippam was fading and JID was beginning to trust his instincts about people. "They're a good crowd. It's a pleasure to meet ordinary people who are not brainwashed by the system. They have strong opinions. Sometimes they disagree yet stay friends. And they are good at chess!"

"Yes, but do you know why?" probed Red.

"They are nice people. Some people naturally get on well with others and some don't. The Chess Club people are real mixers! Anyone would be made really welcome. I haven't seen anything like it for years.

"Yes, but why? Why are they different?"

"I can't think of any other reason. They are just OK. Nice. Civilised."

"You still haven't got it, have you?" roared Red with a loud, genuine yet somehow reassuring laugh. "It's not really anything to do with chess, or OK or nice or civilised. These people are people of truth!"

JID was keen on truth, yet that wasn't a word he would use about the Chess Club! They certainly thought they were true. They wouldn't tell lies about anyone or do any dirty tricks, yet some of their ideas were really strange.

As the conversation went on JID realised that Red actually agreed with these people. Red joined his father and Ruth's in JID's mental list of 'nice but crazy'. He then realised that Ruth, too, should really be in the same category - and that thought hurt him. But Red's whole personality impressed JID. He decided to ask more questions about Red's lifestyle, and listen carefully to the answers. The discussion may well have continued all night, but Red was playing in the match the next day so, at 9.30pm, Red started to make his apologies and ease towards the door. By then JID did not want him to go. He still classed Red as crazy, yet JID was more drawn towards craziness than ever before! Might there be something in this religious stuff?

Red eventually, reached the door. He then, almost as an afterthought, said, "Will you be at the match tomorrow?"

JID said that he applied too late for a ticket and would probably watch the 3Dvid.

"And miss the atmosphere??" shouted Red. JID was not sure if Red was serious or having a laugh with him. "You'd better have one of these."

Red handed a ticket for the VIP Lounge, and headed off down the street.

. . . . .

Again, JID couldn't sleep. Again he spent hours with ideas flowing like the Niagara Falls. This time, however, his mind was far from military or political revolution. This was much more important - it involved the meaning of life and existence. He thought deeply about all that had happened to him that year and the people he had met. When his thoughts got too much for him he found himself praying - then stopped suddenly when he caught himself! He was too logical to be involved in anything like THAT!

He began to think slightly more - and to pray a lot more. Eventually he prayed, "OK boss! What's it all about? I don't think I'm a believer but talking and thinking about you seems cool! So I may try it again when things are rough." JID felt calm, fell into a grin almost as wide as Red's, and was asleep within a minute.

. . . . .

The next day JID got up early as the match kicked off in mid-morning. He wasn't sure if anything had happened to him other than some psychological kick, but the peace he had felt the night before was still there and he walked with a spring in his step. He went to the ground for the match. Instead of walking automatically to his usual part of the ground, he had to carefully follow the signs to the VIP Lounge.

The Lounge was comfort itself. Each person had a seat that he could configure into any shape he felt comfortable with. The view of the pitch was uninterrupted. He realised that the technology meant he could listen to a commentary if he wished by a flick of a switch. (He chose not to use that. It may be new technology that somehow directed some sort of beam directly into the brain - and JID had had too much brainwashing in the Megatrade Convention event.) If anyone asked for a drink or food it would be delivered by some sort of machine, to a tray fixed on the seat, within seconds of the request - and all at the right temperature.

JID asked what the price for the food was, but was told that VIPs didn't have to pay anything. He was feeling peckish so he asked for a hamburger with tomato sauce. The burger arrived immediately. JID then mentioned to the person on his right that he picked the wrong sauce, he really wanted a brown sauce. His comment was not aimed at the machine - he would be content with tomato sauce, but the machine whisked the burger away and replaced it with a burger and brown sauce.

JID looked around the people in the Lounge. They looked like other people - all shapes and sizes, although there were, not surprisingly, a fair proportion of people who were physically fit. They included retired players and a few players who were generally fit, but were carrying an injury. He then realised that he was sat next to Jason 'The Shot' Shotton, scorer of 43 goals for Merziblu five seasons earlier, just before he retired. What would the genius think about his choice of food?

JID said, "Hello, Jason. I didn't recognise you at first. Can I have your autograph?"

Jason duly obliged - and asked JID if he was an Merzibluian. "No, I'm from Northampton", replied JID, "but I know Red from years ago and he got me a ticket for this Lounge - very plush too by my normal standards! I still remember that game when you hit four against Manchester United. The defenders had no idea how to stop you!

Jason appeared very modest and just said he had a lucky day and was helped by the rainy conditions.

After a discussion about Jason's football career there was a roar from the crowd as the players took to the field. Red gave a wave to the Merziblu supporters end, to the cameras and then in the direction of the VIP Lounge. As usual play started fifteen minutes late to fit in with the 3Dvid schedules and megacompany adverts. Northampton started well and were denied a goal by Red when he dived full length to head what seemed a certain goal off the line. "Red in blue, Red in blue...", chanted the Merziblu supporters. JID's mind drifted from the football for a moment as he realised that Merziblu were the only top team that still played in its traditional colours despite the controlling grip of the 'Friendly Sponsors' who seemed to have their way in demanding the colours of all the other teams. Merziblu was able and determined enough to remain individualistic.

The game was an exciting one, but the score was still 0-0. Northampton played well and matched Merziblu for a lot of the play. Half-time refreshments were automatically provided once again, and after JID had had a toilet break he started to chat with Jason once again. He mentioned that Red seemed to have a philosophy that made him happy but not mindless. He asked if Jason knew why.

JID found himself able to talk more freely than he had for years. He was not quite sure why this should be. Was he in a half-drunk state after what had happened last night, or perhaps it was the euphoria he often felt when he was at a match. "What do you think about the state of NWE just now", he asked.

Jason said it was the best for a decade! "Jim Haynes of Liverpool and Red make a powerful link between defence and attack. Tim Northall, the Merziblu goalkeeper, was one of the most reliable on Earth and NWE had at least three forwards who could get behind the defence."

"I agree," said JID, "but what about the political situation? And the social situation? And the religious situation?"

Jason stood up and walked away from his seat. JID realised that he was deliberately walking away from the seats as they were more likely to be bugged. "Political and social? Just look around you! Most people have no interest or aim in life. If you can still think for yourself and even ask questions like the one you asked, proves that you are one of the lucky ones who still have a brain. You are also one of the unlucky ones who will be on every official wanted list the Government and the companies produce. Religion? I don't take to it myself, but they've really got some courage. I'm not talking about the official religion of course, any moron can follow that - and a lot of them do. I'm talking about the traditionalists. They don't want to be led up the garden path by Joe King and his merry men. If you want to know more there is a rumour that quite a few of the players and directors of Merziblu are now into, so you are in the right place to find out more, but it's not my thing.

Again, there was a roar from the crowd as the players took to the pitch, and Jason and JID took their seats. Merziblu made a tactical change and now took the initiative. An extra defender was brought on in place of a forward, but Red was given a freer role to look for gaps. In the fourth minute of the second half Red took a free kick from 30 metress out and almost cracked the crossbar. He continued to be the mastermind behind Merziblu as they took control. He made a goal for the striker in the 53$^{rd}$ minute and won a corner in the 63$^{rd}$ that led to Merziblu's second goal. In the 76$^{th}$ minute Red dribbled the ball 40 metres, beat three defenders and thundered a shot past the goalkeeper from twenty yards. As he unleashed his shot one of the defenders put his knee where it hurt Red most and Red was carried off. Those watching on 3Dvid heard that Lipcom interpreted Red's comment as "Man, you shouldn't have done that. My wife will be disappointed! But I'll try to forgive you!"

Just before the end of stoppage time Red appeared in the VIP Lounge, walking very stiffly. JID offered him his seat, which Red was happy to accept.

"I bet you'll bury that defender next time you play!" said JID.

"No, I'll try not to," said the Red who had changed since school days. "I can't remember what I said to him, but I hope that it wasn't too violent!"

"We'll see what the recorded highlights say tonight," grinned JID. He then asked if Red had some time to chat before he left Northampton. Red said that he could stay a day or two as he had been advised by the physio not to go near another football for at least three days. They went to a restaurant and Red paid for the meal. The conversation was stilted as both felt the presence of unseen 3Dvid cameras. When they got to JID's flat they felt freer to speak.

As the conversation continued, JID became more and more convinced that Red's traditional religion was right! He couldn't understand why. It didn't fit with what he had learned at school or even what his parents said to him before they had changed - but it seemed right. He peppered Red with all kinds of questions about how his way of thinking fitted in with other theories and philosophies. Red didn't seem to have quite the same wide philosophical knowledge that JID had, but that didn't seem to matter. He could answer every question with a calm confidence that was rare in JID's experience, even before the collapse of sanity in the nation - and that at a time when Red was still in a state of physical pain from the football injury.

They stopped talking to watch 'Today's Football' on 3Dvid. When Red scored his goal he flinched at the thought of the tackle on his tackle, and JID felt sick as he hadn't realised quite how bad it was from his position in the luxury of the VIP Lounge. The four ex-players who assessed the games did a special feature on Red Young who had suffered what they called an 'unfortunate accident'. The 3Dvid of the game proved to Red and JID that it was actually a very deliberate attempt to put Red out of football for a long period. When Lipcom told them what Red had said they both burst out laughing.

JID let Red use the bed and he arranged cushions on the floor to sleep on. JID was tired. He thought for a moment, said "OK, God! You win." He then fell soundly asleep.

. . . . .

JID got up early the next morning. He considered how he got where he was. Had he really decided to go traditional? Was it his idea? Had somebody prayed for it? Could their prayers make any difference? Or had he been caught up in another elaborate mind-bending trick? The more he thought about it, the more convinced he was that all was well.

He remained deliriously happy even when he thought about his not-yet-started relationship with Ruth. He could see that she had been right to avoid talk of marriage before he had reached this stage. His life was completely monopolised, yet he was confident that he was really free for the first time in his life. While he felt even more madly in love with Ruth, he knew that even this love would always be the second most important when he considered God's love. He also recognised that her plans may diverge from his as they considered where life would take them in these uncertain times.

He tried to record a 3Dvid to Ruth. He was deliriously happy, but nervous at the same time. He decided to type the message, but his fingers trembled on the keys so it took him six attempts before he got it right.

"Hi, Ruth. I'm going to be completely truthful with you- although the truth is not the same as it was yesterday! First, I am as much in love with you as I have ever been. No, that's not right! I know you and understand you and love you miles more than ever.

"But there's something else you should know. I got to know your friend Red Young and he introduced me to his friend Jesus. You'll be glad to know that it all makes sense to me now! I've even been forgiven for hating Mighty Malc and the morons who agreed with him at that Liverpool happening I told you about.

"I think that I have changed so much that I am not the same person and may be over the top even for you! If I have to choose between you and this faith, I'd have to say that I will keep my faith.

JID then hastened to add, "I still love you, but will you love me?"

JID didn't know how he would feel when he sent the 3Dvid to Ruth, but he felt light as a feather after he told the computer to "Send."

. . . . .

Red gingerly descended the stairs. JID sat him at the table and prepared breakfast. JID told Red about all that had happened and Red was delighted. For several hours they discussed it and what it would all mean.

Then Red took out a chart of exercises he had promised the physio he would do to ease his suffering and get himself back into the team soon.

JID went to his screen and saw there was a brief 3Dvid message from Ruth. "Where have you been? I've been trying to contact you for hours. That's great news you sent. Let's fix a date for the wedding!"

# Chapter 6. June.
# The Crunch and the Aftermath...

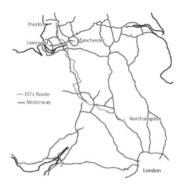

"Frack away", yelled the foreman, and a huge explosion underground was triggered six kilometres from the McCallow's home in Hesketh Bank. They decided to frack an hour earlier than usual as a serious thunderstorm was brewing.

Fracking had been very controversial when it started in the area. It was a commercial technique that used explosives to release natural gas for collection and use. The gas was pumped straight into the NWE gas grid reservoirs and heated homes all over the country.

The system hadn't been without controversy. There had been the usual round of pressure groups and petitions. In the period before Parliament lost all credibility, local MP's expressed serious concerns about fracking in the area. All that was now history and fracking was a profitable part of the local economy, which everyone knew about and few bothered to oppose because they knew that no amount of pressure could ever stop or reduce it.

. . . . .

JID had been to Preston to visit Ruth for the last two weekends and after work once each week. His love for her grew more and more, and they worked on the details of the wedding. As there was now no official records of weddings it made the organisation simpler. They talked with each set of parents about their plans and the whole thing seemed to fall into place. The date was set for the first weekend in July.

JID had wondered what Jules Barnet had envisaged when he was silenced by the TV gurus. Could the whole transport system grind to a halt? Would the failing economy be much harder hit by a technological failure? He tried not to think about it too much especially when he depended on it to see Ruth.

Despite the intellectual and moral murk of the nation, and despite his problems at the hands of the companies he felt at peace and well looked after. He saw the news and the state of the world, but (for now at least) everything was beautiful.

He had worked a couple of extra hours on Monday and Tuesday so that he could have Wednesday afternoon off to see Ruth. He'd got up early so that he would be able to see all the news on 3Dvid as he was eating his breakfast.

. . . . .

Southport was a former holiday resort in Greater Merseyside, about 30 kilometres north of Liverpool. It remained a pleasant place to live and work. When gravity-reversal became possible there was much debate about where the international central control rooms would be situated. Southport was the natural centre. It was an area that produced many very talented people and was also a pleasant area for capable technicians and technocrats to move to. The main building on a previously undeveloped site just beyond the north east of the town, near the Ribble estuary, was just two storeys high as the unstable subsoil made higher buildings expensive, so instead of building high, the buildings spread over many acres.

The only higher structure was the perimeter wall surrounding the transmitters. It was 25 metres high to hide the unsightly view from discerning residents. It was also 30 metres from the nearest transmitter so that even in the unlikely event of the wall collapsing the transmitters would be undamaged.

A series of similar stations sprouted around the globe, about 1,000 kilometres apart, but, since the Southport Centre was the first to be developed anywhere, it had also become the international centre. All the centres dealt with traffic in a vast area, each making it possible for the transporters to stay aloft. If a centre suddenly went off-line it could cause disasters in their area, but the regions beyond would be unaffected. However, all the regional centres needed to be coordinated from a single international centre, which software would make sure that collisions would be impossible because the centres would work together.

Naturally, for such a sensitive installation, safety features were paramount. The proximity of the fracking, less than ten kilometres away from the Southport centre had been taken into account. The area was never troubled by natural earthquakes, but even an industrial earthquake caused by fracking would not be able to cause any damage. The specially designed transmitters had gyroscopic correctors, which combined with local radio signals and satnav systems. Any movement of the transmitters would be corrected within 0.014 of a second, and the transporters would not even change course enough for the passengers to notice.

In the experimental period, transporters were made to fly at various speeds, up to twice the normal speed, over the Irish Sea. A huge artificial earthquake was caused and over a thousand houses in Southport were damaged, some seriously, but the transporters flew as intended.

The system had worked successfully for four years and had caused no problem whatsoever, in any part of the world.

. . . . .

The adverts finished and Phantom Smith's turn came around.

"Hello, Phantom Smith reporting." He stood facing JID. "Late last night we heard about the resumption of the trial of Evangelical Christians in the United States".

The scene changed and JID was in the courtroom facing the defendants. Smith's voice continued, "The 29 defendants have been warned that any reference to divinity of any kind is illegal and unconstitutional! They had been warned that it could result in solitary confinement for two weeks..."

JID thought about the broadcast. There had been just 28 people on trial, so where had the other come from? He walked into the 3Dvid and from one side he could just about see the face of Maurice Ruggers, the son of another defendant. Maurice had tried to present a legal case on their behalf. He was now in chains like his father and the others. JID's attention went back to the broadcast, in time to hear the judge declare, "You have violated international law and the two most recent amendments to the American Constitution. It is to your shame that congress and representatives have both had to meet to pass these amendments in the last few days to prevent your behaviour from going unpunished. This and any future blasphemy against Worldfaith will be severely punished. I am a compassionate man, and hesitate to use the death penalty, so you will all be locked up for the whole of your lives.

The inevitable advert break followed, which gave JID time to put the dishes in the dishwasher and get a second cup of tea. When he started to return to the sitting room with tea in hand, the house shook and he was thrown off his feet. There was a loud noise, though it was more like a drawn out rumble than an explosion. He went to the tap to put cold water on his scalded hand, but the water system had been damaged. He saw that the pipe had ruptured near the ceiling on the other side of the room, so he bathed his hand under the pipe and then ran to turn the water off at the mains before too much damage was done.

JID fell back into the chair. The adverts were expected to last several more minutes. The advert on the screen at the time flashed, and parts of it could only be seen on the 2Dvid screen in the corner. At the end of the advert a very frightened Phantom Smith appeared. "Early reports say that earthquakes all over the country have rocked the homes of most people. Our own studios in Liverpool have been damaged by flying wreckage. There are already reports of problems from Thurso to Penzance. We are not yet sure how much damage has been done. While some buildings have been badly damaged, particularly in city centres, many more rural areas seem almost untouched.

JID was disorientated, but the local transporter he had booked to get him to work was due to arrive in five minutes so, despite his shaking, he got ready to leave. He went out of his flat and waited.

And waited!

When it was clear that his transport was unlikely to arrive he started to walk the two miles to the office. He turned the first corner and saw the cause of the quake near his home. A medium sized long-distance transporter had crashed and demolished a house. JID saw that one or two people were feverishly hand digging so he ran home and collected his wheelbarrow and a couple of sturdy shovels. He and a total of five others worked like slaves to reach the people in the house. A woman who was working with JID told him that a couple with a ten year old boy lived there. They needed to find them to get medical attention for them.

Another group had already looked at the wreckage of the transporter to find just one man alive, and they were doing what they could for him while they waited for the transportivance to take him to the hospital. They expected it any moment as the news programmes had recently told the nation that anyone, anywhere in NEW, would never have to wait more than 8 minutes from the time of a call to the National Transportivance Service, and they would be at the local hospital in a further six minutes.

A crowd of people had gathered to watch the dig, so JID yelled, "Stop looking and come and give us a hand!"

Nobody moved, but they just looked on with their mouths open. He tried again, "Just get moving, lives are at stake here!"

There was a slight movement in the crowd, but not in the right direction. Some members of the crowd turned and walked away. Meanwhile JID and the others kept digging. After about half an hour JID and the workers found two bodies, but the mother was still alive.

JID phoned for a transportivance, but was told, "We are sorry that there is an exceptionally high demand for transportivances today. If a transportivance has been ordered for your area, please be patient as each transportivance can treat and carry at least six casualties…."

JID was frustrated and furious. He interrupted, "We have got dangerously injured people here!".

He then heard his vidphone say "This is a recorded message. Normal service will resume as soon as possible. Have a nice day!"

JID groaned at this meaningless American expression, and turned to assess the situation. The woman who had spoken to JID earlier turned out to be a qualified emergency nurse, and she was tending the woman they had rescued. The transportivance had still not appeared for the man injured in the transporter. JID and the others had to cope on their own. He went home and there was still plenty of water in the kettle. He made as many cups of tea and coffee as he could. He just about managed to get to the wreckage before some of the mindless spectators were able to get to him and steal the drinks. All the ones who had been working appreciated the drinks and drank them quickly.

The condition of the mother rescued from the house worsened. JID tried dialling 999, then the transportivance number, then 999 and 911. In each case he got exactly the same message as before. It was impossible to get through to anyone who could help in any way. 'Why, oh why can't anyone in the emergency services do their jobs?' thought JID.

After a further ten minutes JID and a couple of other rescuers came close to the woman in pain, trying to comfort her. Then she asked, in a barely audible voice, "Are any of you traditional Christians?"

Instantly JID and all the other rescuers said, "Yes, me," and they were all as surprised as each other. The injured girl said, "My husband has recently been into the old religion at the Drama Club. What's it all about?"

One of the other men there explained and led a prayer with her and the others. She gave a genuine, happy smile and said, "Thank you, I understand now," and she shut her eyes, slept for a few moments breathing peacefully and then died.

The others were sad for her, but they exchanged their 3Dvid numbers and promised to contact each other.

The man injured in the transporter was making good progress, so JID realised that his contribution to the immediate disaster was not so urgently needed. He realised that he would be unlikely to be able to get to Preston that evening so he called Ruth on 3Dphone.

Ruth looked relieved to see him. "Why haven't you returned my calls?" she asked. "I assumed you must have died in a transporter." She then looked at the screen and shouted, "Are you alright? You look like you were in an accident!"

"No, don't worry. The accident was a few streets away. I helped the relief work, but it's all OK now. Anyway, how is my favourite lady?"

"I'm OK, but a lot of people have died here."

"Died? Why?" asked JID. Then he remembered the report from the news earlier. "Oh, sorry, I was thinking that this was the only disaster. What has happened? What is the news of the earthquake?"

Again Ruth showed her amazing grasp of many subjects. "I think the official announcements and the truth are very different. I've listened to the news a few times and they are talking about a volcano in Holland causing quakes in NWE and the Western continent. But I think that it is failure to listen to Jules Barnet! My father is a close friend of Jules." (JID was fascinated, but not really surprised.) "He knew that Jules was trying to alert everyone to the danger of transporters if earthquakes and electrical storms happened at the same time. (That often happens in areas prone to earthquakes, but since most earthquake areas were a long way away the Government didn't care). Jules had information that this situation could be deadly. I 3Dvided Dad after I tried to contact you and he said that he had heard a bang just after a transporter crashed, but that was immediately followed by an explosion from the fracking."

"So it must have been explosives at the fracking plant that caused the earthquake." JID said.

"NO", said Ruth! "It takes several seconds for the sounds to reach Preston! We had a thunderstorm here just after. When the explosion happened the air was highly charged and the whole scenario developed."

"So you think that if they had listened to Jules Barnet it could have been alright?"

"I'm sure of it", Ruth responded, "then the transporters crashed".

. . . . . . . . . . . . . . . .

JID was unable to go to work the next day - he was shocked and weakened. He was in regular contact with Ruth by 3Dvid, but the transport system had failed completely. He 'phoned the office to apologise, but there was no answer. Had other people in the office been shocked by what they saw? Or perhaps it was even worse - maybe some or all had died in accidents during the rush hour that morning.

What he didn't realise at the time was that it was not just NWE that was suffering! All of the civilised world lost their only usable transport system. Many roads and railways had been plundered (by opportunists or officially by the Governments or owners). Lots of the sites had been built on, especially after the loss of many millions of square kilometres in many lands about the time of the floods that devastated London. Some roads, of course, remained but the problem people faced was the lack of vehicles. In the rush to provide transporter stock the price of metal hit the roof and owners of vehicles were happy to sell them and use conventional public transport in the few months before there were enough transporters to go round. Now, at a stroke, the transporter system had, literally, collapsed.

JID was going to find the extent of the problems in the next week or so. That day he got home he had something to eat and went to bed early. He felt tired enough even though it was just late afternoon. But first, he wanted to catch up with the state of the world and then speak with friends.

He turned on the 3Dvid. Only the 2D screen worked, but that was better than nothing. He was greeted by the usual sickening range of megacompany propaganda. The news should have started 12 minutes ago, so he knew that the actual start time could be imminent. He got another shock when Phantom Smith appeared. Smith was calm and collected with none of the panic that was so obvious the last time JID saw the news.

"Today is a wonderful day!" he beamed.

'Is this guy in the same country as the rest of us?' thought JID.

"The going is soft to firm for the June meeting at Ayr racecourse. The favourite for the day's last race, Criminy Jicket, has very short odds, but many still think it a good bet at 5 to 2. Personally, I will be backing Fly Paper at a generous 15 to 1..."

At that, JID realised something must be wrong. He had put £300 at 15 to 1 on Fly Paper the previous year in the same race, and won. He rarely betted and he really enjoyed the result. He could afford to go in the centre stand the next time he went to see Northampton play. That win stuck in his mind because in its next race two weeks later Fly Paper was injured at a jump and had to be shot.

The companies must have put out last year's news in the hope that nobody noticed. The sad thing was that many didn't notice, and the bookmaker branch of all the megacompany stores that managed to open took nearly ten billion pounds for Fly Paper to win at 15 to 1!

Today's real news was clearly off limits for the general public! JID tried to switch off, but the screen continued to give bland, recycled news. The 'off' switch was defunct - and not just in JID's flat!

He contacted Ruth to see how she was coping. The loud background noise was the same as in his flat. The Prime Minister was waxing lyrical about improvements to the television system and the introduction of 3Dvid - another 'great achievement' of the partnership between companies and Government.

"Hi, love. What is the world like at your end?" asked Ruth.

"Grim," he replied, and went on to give a full roundup of events so far.

Ruth then described her day, which was remarkably similar to JID's and many other peoples'. Her flat had been damaged by wreckage from the sky, but the bedroom was still habitable. JID's parents had provided meals for her as her kitchen was beyond immediate repair. They had offered to put her up for the night, but she said she would try to cope at her own flat for the first night and see how it went. (The damage was worse than she thought so she moved in with JID's parents after the first night.)

She was too weak to pull people from the rubble, but she had spent the day providing food and a messaging service for the ones doing the work. She told him that the biggest problem was trying to get jobs done when so many people stood around and got in the way. The emergency services were as efficient in Preston as they had been in Northampton.

After about half an hour telling their sad tales they finished their conversations and blew each other kisses. Even that didn't seem as good as it was in 3D.

Next he talked to his parents and Ruth's. They, like Ruth, had been busy helping at disaster scenes. They, too, saw few survivors from the transporters or on the ground. By the grace of God none of his close family had suffered physically, although the whole event had naturally had a huge negative affect on them all.

There was one thing he was glad about. They all wanted the wedding to go ahead despite the day's events.

The last people he 'phoned were the ones he had met at the disaster scene. He was glad that he had met so many Christians who lived close to him. He and they would benefit from each other's company in the days ahead.

. . . . .

The next few days were difficult for JID. His midweek visit to Ruth had been prevented and there were technological problems that made it more and more difficult to contact her at all. It was several days since he had seen her face, and voice-only calls became less frequent as the exchanges did not work all of the time.

Each day seemed the same for JID. He would get up each morning and try to contact work. He would walk to his office to see if anyone was there, and nobody was. He would trudge the two miles home and stop off at the home of John and Joan Yada for their company and prayers. (They had been among the helpers after the transporter crash). Some of the other workers who helped at the disaster were there. Another person there was Ed Jerton, the man who had been rescued from the transporter. In the absence of medical help he was being nursed back to health by John and Joan. He had been single since the death of his partner two years earlier and had no close family.

JID had appreciated the Yada's support, and looked to them for advice. They had encouraged him to start to try to get to Preston. He hadn't for two reasons. He wanted to be there when his office started to work again, and he still hoped that some kind of transport system would materialise.

Eventually he decided that the Yadas were right. He went to their house and thanked them for their help and concern for him. When he told them, they prayed with him and gave him their best wishes. Just as he was leaving, John asked him to stay a few more minutes while he made some calls. "I've had an idea", said John. "Stay with us a while longer and have something to eat, while I try to do something to make life easier for you."

John came back into the sitting room and sat down. Over the inevitable drone of the news on 2Dvid he said that the idea had paid off.

JID asked what the idea was, but John just said, "All will be revealed."

JID was impatient to start to walk, but, out of respect for his friend, he sat as patiently as he could.

The screen suddenly fell silent, and John, Joan and JID all expressed relief. Their relief didn't last long as they realised that the cooker had also ceased to function and they would lose the half-cooked joint in the oven. All power was off!

Soon there was a knock at the door, and Len Jenkins was invited in. John introduced him to JID. Len was a friend of the Yadas who sang in the South Northampton Choir with Joan. He had been the owner of a large local cycle shop, one of the few that hadn't been absorbed into a megacompany when the transporter revolution happened. He sold half of his bikes for the metal and made a fortune, but he kept a few as souvenirs, including five rugged mountain bikes for practical use. His family had one each and one was spare. He had ridden to John's house on the spare bike to give it to JID. JID insisted that he would pay something towards it, but Len absolutely refused. He was very well off and was glad to help.

JID rode to his flat to collect his tent and other things he would need and loaded the large panniers on the bike. He then set out on the long ride toward Preston. That journey was to be much more eventful than JID ever expected. He did not realise that it was the last time he would ever see Northampton. He set off towards the M45 and the M6. He knew that they would probably be free from traffic - he hadn't seen any surface transport for four or five years. The journey was a lot slower than it would have been. There were several points where he had to get off the bike to find a way over or around wreckage from transporter accidents.

His plan to use the motorways backfired. The part on the M45 was eventless, but when he was ten minutes into his ride on the M6 he heard a rumbling noise behind him at a distance, getting louder. He gathered that it must be heavy vehicles of some kind and that he would be safer away from it. He stopped by the side of the road on top of an embankment. The traffic coming from behind him was a large convoy of what seemed to be military vehicles. When the first vehicle was about 200 metres away he heard gunshots. He thought that he may be the intended target and dived down the embankment. As the vehicles drove past him a loudspeaker from one of the vehicles roared out, "No civilian transport may use Motorways or 'A' roads until further notice."

JID got up and dusted himself off. When the last vehicle in the convoy disappeared he climbed the embankment to check and collect his bike. There had been no damage when he dropped the bike and he would be able to ride it.

Near the bottom of the embankment was a country lane, and it was clear of traffic and pedestrians, so he carried the bike down the embankment, crossed the ditch at the bottom and climbed the fence before he dragged the bike behind him. He ripped his waterproof jacket on the barbed wire. After a trudge through a muddy field he was relieved to be able to climb on his bike again and set off parallel to the motorway at about 30kph.

He then realised a problem. He stopped and took out the map he was carrying only to discover that it only showed motorways and major roads, the ones that were now barred from civilian use. It was now late afternoon so he tried to make sure that he was riding with the sun on his left hand side. He came to a village where he decided to try to get lodgings. When he asked the first person he met, he found that he was regarded as a threat. Nobody would speak to an outsider. He managed to buy some food from them, at about twice the normal price, and slept outdoors in his tent about a kilometre from the village.

He kept in touch with Ruth by 'phone, with short calls for a couple of days, in an effort to save the battery, but soon found that he was unable to continue 'phoning. He didn't know if that was caused by his battery running out or by a general collapse of communications. When he eventually reached Preston he realised that it was the latter.

Under normal circumstances he would be able to ride the distance from Northampton to Preston in about three or four days but this time it took much longer. He eventually arrived after eight days of hard riding on badly battered roads. Food was scarce and becoming scarcer. People were becoming more frightened and less cooperative. Many roads had been built over, or were banned for civilian use, or had been damaged by crashing transporters.

He found out which road had been the M6, which goes near Preston, and rode on smaller roads roughly parallel to it, so he knew that he was going in the right direction.

He had already been told that Ruth was staying at his parents' house so he went straight there. They had a wonderful reunion and retired to different rooms, but not before JID had had a well-earned shower.

The next day JID decided it was time to catch up on the news, which was now on the usual channels, but only in sound, not even 2Dvid. This time there was some genuine news!

The first thing Phantom Smith said was, "We have some grave news from Western Asia. Our spy satellites have detected movement of the forces travelling southwards between the Caspian Sea and the Black Sea. The forces cover several hundred square kilometres. After the Israeli threat they had stopped moving southwards, but now they have continued their advance.

"Despite our truce with our Arab neighbours," the President of Israel declared, "we are facing a huge threat. As I said in the last few months, we will respond vigorously to any breach of our sovereignty. We face twin threats. One threat is the growing numbers of underground Christian groups that are now about 24% of our population. They are causing general political nervousness in the country.

The second is caused by Arab nations in our area who are beginning to renege on their peace deal, which has lasted over three years."

Phantom Smith's voice returned, "China has said that they do not know the purpose of the build-up of forces, but that their forces are now crossing Iraq and expect to arrive soon. And now a word from our sponsors...

. . . . .

When the sports news started, JID tried to turn off, but failed. He wondered what was the point or the meaning of sport under the circumstances that were unfolding? Or would they just produce ancient or fictitious news?

He asked Ruth if she had heard from Red Young or his wife recently, but she said "No". He said that he would phone them, still unaware that that any form of personal electronic communication was either banned or impossible due to the complete breakdown of communications. Ruth put him in the picture.

# Chapter 7. July.
# The Bliss of the Wedding...

JID sat nervously in the front row, on the first floor of the building that was formerly the home of the Labour Club in Preston. He reflected on the crazy few months that he had just experienced. The vast majority of the survivors were terrified and jumpy. JID was nervous for a very different reason than the rest! The more he thought about things the happier and more confident he became. All of life became a difficult challenge, but he was enjoying every minute.

All the plans for the wedding had had to be changeable. Nothing could be predicted about life. The original idea was to have the wedding in the Chess Club, but the plans were demolished with the Chess Club when the gravity-reversal transporters crashed. One of the people in the Club had been a member of the Labour Club before it closed when normal political life collapsed. He and a conservative both offered the keys to their clubs, and there had been some leg-pulling about whether the Church should consider itself socialist or capitalist. Mark had said (with a grin) that the Labour Club was better equipped for games of chess - so that is where they ended up.

The wedding was to be in the large upstairs auditorium. As soon as they moved into the Labour Club they arranged a warning light to warn of any intrusion of suspected spies. When the electricity failed they arranged a pulley system instead. A pull of a rope downstairs caused black and white flags to drop over the front and back of the room. A pull on another rope withdrew the flags. Since the Club had moved they had been untroubled by the authorities - but they were taking no chances.

Oli Timson had been a loud mouthed but hard working assistant in a general store. He could cause an argument in an empty room, although he was quite likeable. He had inherited the shop when the owner, a 90 year old spinster died. Despite becoming a small time capitalist by default, he maintained his socialist sympathies. He was a former member of the Labour Club and he decided to make a fuss about the Chess Club taking the building without paying rent. (Actually Mark had tried very hard to find anybody who had any responsibility for the disused and decaying building but was unsuccessful at the time). Oli was welcomed and looked after by the Chess Club members because he had lost his home. They made a spare room comfortable for him to stay in and made sure he had enough to eat. He thought that he had been looked after just because they were trying to stop him making a fuss, when he was introduced to former wealthy industrialist Ed Mannier, who had lost everything, including his wife and children, when London was flooded. Ed's flat in Preston had suffered the same fate as Oli's. After discussing (and disagreeing about) outdated politics for the best part of an hour Oli found out that Ed's current home was in the room next to his.

Oli and Ed had, since moving in, begun to realise why the Chess Club people were different to the rest. They had both been reluctant to be persuaded simply by the generosity of the Chess Club people, but, as they talked and listened with them, they realised that they had the only real explanation of the situation and their baptisms were planned for just after JID and Ruth's wedding.

JID thought of them and smiled, comparing it to his own new life. Life was not easy and it certainly would not improve in the immediate future, but he was blissfully happy. So were Oli and Ed and all who had had the guts to go Christian. It was difficult to get the normal things of life. Food, soap and toilet paper, for instance, were rare and expensive. Some people had hoarded supplies and were making a financial killing. Some Christians had built up their supplies, but were now happy to share what they had with the others. That meant that the wedding, even though it did not include the huge feast that had been normal a decade earlier, was a happy social event.

Many people had contributed to the wedding in all kinds of different ways. Both JID's suit and Ruth's wedding dress had been given by guests. Ruth's mother had kept her wedding dress in perfect condition, although it was slightly too large for Ruth. A Chess Club member had adjusted it perfectly, and had made the bridesmaid's dress.

JID had decided that he wouldn't have a best man. His close friends in Northampton were either dead or completely prevented from travelling by the situation. Red Young would have been his choice, but he had no way of knowing where Red and Kit were, or even if they were dead or alive. He knew several people in the Chess Club, but none well enough to ask to be the best man.

He looked at his watch - it was about 20 minutes to go. He wished that Ruth would appear and the wedding would go ahead. Nervousness began to creep in again, so he again basked in the thought that he and Ruth would be together as long as they lived.

He could hear the bustle of guests arriving. He decided to walk around and see the guests who had already walked upstairs. He had greeted all of them when he heard cheering from below. He thought that Ruth must have arrived, when suddenly Red Young appeared from the stairway!

"Red!! It's great to see you! I didn't know you were going to be able to get here! How have you coped recently. Is Kit OK? Where are you staying? What's the news from your angle? How have..."

Red butted in, "Calm down, there'll be time for all that later. Kit is at Mark's house with Ruth, and Ruth asked her to be a lady-of-honour. When we went to the house, they invited us to the wedding, and I believe that you need a best man! I would like to apply for the job."

"Application happily accepted!" said JID.

The wedding march started and the congregation stood up. No electronic instrument could be used, but a guitar and an old grand piano broke into the traditional 'Here comes the bride'. The piano had been specially tuned for the occasion by a musical Chess Club member. He had never tuned a piano in his life before, but he made an excellent job of it and the piano sounded magnificent.

JID looked over his shoulder to see Ruth, who looked even more beautiful than ever, and JID couldn't stop himself from suddenly crying bucketsful of tears of joy. When she was nearly at the front Red whispered to JID, "You're supposed to stand up!"

JID sheepishly did as he was told and joined the rest of the congregation who were already on their feet.

The notice board outside the Labour Club declared that it was a lecture on Chess Tactics, to confuse anyone from the megacompanies, if the megacompanies still existed. (Nobody seemed sure). The service would be based on the previous service book, although Mark had discussed it with JID and Ruth - and they made some changes. They also understood that they would use their common sense if the black-and-white flag appeared. The King and Queen would represent JID and Ruth! God Almighty would be 'The Player'.

He then started by saying, "Dearly beloved, we are gathered together here in the sight of God, and in the face of this congregation, to join together this man and this woman in the honourable estate of holy matrimony."

JID, Ruth and the whole congregation fell about laughing at this introduction. It was so uncharacteristic for Mark to talk like that. When the laughter subsided, he continued...

"Don't worry! I'm not going to continue in 1662AD language! I'm just using it to show that what we are doing has been accepted as good and proper for many generations. Our generation has been trying to destroy marriage, but well done to JID and Ruth for having the courage and the joy of recognising God's part in their hearts and in their unity."

There was a round of applause and cheering at these words, with JID and Ruth clapping the loudest. Mark held up his hand for silence so that he could continue with a Bible verse:

"God is love, and those who live in love live in God and God lives in them."

Then he prayed: "Send your Holy Spirit, and pour into our hearts that most excellent gift of love, through Jesus Christ our Lord. Amen.

"In the presence of God, Father, Son and Holy Spirit, we have come together to witness the marriage of JID and Ruth, to pray for God's blessing on them, to share their joy and to celebrate their love.

"Marriage is a gift of God in creation through which husband and wife may know the grace of God.

"Christ is united with his bride, the Church. That is the model for our marriages! May there be joyful commitment until the end of their lives. May they find strength, companionship and comfort, and grow to maturity in love. It is a sign of unity and loyalty.

"It should be undertaken reverently and responsibly in the sight of almighty God.

"JID and Ruth are now to enter this way of life. But first, I am required to ask anyone present who knows a reason why these persons may not UNLAWFULLY marry, to declare it now."

He deliberately stressed the word 'unlawfully' because everyone there knew the law, and possible consequences of being at that wedding. When he had finished the question there was a rumbling noise, but it wasn't words of complaint! It was the entire congregation joining in with loud applause!

Mark continued, "If either of you knows a reason why you may not marry, you must declare it now."

He looked at JID,
"JID will you take my beautiful daughter Ruth to be your wife?
Will you love her, comfort her, honour and protect her, and, forsaking all others,
be faithful to her as long as you both shall live?

JID shouted, "Sure will!"

Mark turned to Ruth,
"Ruth, this sensible man, JID wants you to be his wife!
Will you take JID to be your husband?
Will you love him, comfort him, honour and protect him,
and, forsaking all others,
be faithful to him as long as you both shall live?

Ruth beamed and shouted almost as loudly as JID "Ab-so-lute-ly!"

Mark looked up to the congregation, "Will you, the families and friends of JID and Ruth support and uphold them in their marriage?

The congregation shouted "Yes," and started to clap again.

JID's father, Nigel Davies, stood up to do the Bible reading:

> "If I speak in the tongues of men and of angels, but have not love, I am only a resounding gong or a clanging cymbal. If I have the gift of

prophecy and can fathom all mysteries and all knowledge, and if I have a faith that can move mountains, but have not love, I am nothing. If I give all I possess to the poor and surrender my body to the flames, but have not love, I gain nothing.

Love is patient, love is kind. It does not envy, it does not boast, it is not proud. It is not rude, it is not self-seeking, it is not easily angered, it keeps no record of wrongs. Love does not delight in evil, but rejoices with the truth. It always protects, always trusts, always hopes, always perseveres.

Love never fails. But where there are prophecies, they will cease; where there are tongues, they will be stilled; where there is knowledge, it will pass away. For we know in part and we prophesy in part, but when perfection comes, the imperfect disappears.

When I was a child, I talked like a child, I thought like a child, I reasoned like a child. When I became a man, I put childish ways behind me. Now we see but a poor reflection as in a mirror; then we shall see face to face. Now I know in part; then I shall know fully, even as I am fully known. And now these three remain: faith, hope and love. But the greatest of these is love."

As soon as the reading finished and the sermon was due to start, the black-and-white flags fell loose from the ceiling. A man had stumbled into the building smelling of methylated spirits, but the doorman, Ed Mannier, took no chances. The visitor might have been a spy, just acting drunk.

JID and Ruth sat down and people gathered round Ruth and her entourage so that they would not be so obvious to the spy in the building. Mark started to speak.

"I'm happy to say that my daughter is good when it comes to a match! She is excellent on her own but in chess mixed doubles she has selected a wonderful partner! I am sure that they will be guided by the Spirit of the one who created the game and the brains of all players!

The visitor climbed the stairs clumsily and noisily. "I love lectures", he said, before seating himself on the only spare seat near the aisle. "Tell me all about chests! This is the chest club!"

Many speakers would be put off by this, but Mark continued calmly, "I could talk about chests. Men like women's chests - and that is the way it should be. Even the King and Queen would agree (if we still had kings and queens). It's all about how things are handled. The King, I mean the bigger King- the Player, controls the better part of today's game. What do you all think?"

The congregation started to applaud.

"In the Chess Club we still have kings and queens, as this game proves so magnificently. They will combine in a way that's guided by the player with great skill! After so many years and countless matches he remains matchless.

"Towards the end of the game the teamwork between king and queen becomes even more vital - and we never know just how long the game will continue as we now understand things. The king becomes a more active, attacking piece making bold moves and working for and with the queen. Occasionally the queen makes a sacrifice for the king and the whole team. This works best when mating is imminent - as it surely is here! If we were able to use the 3Dvid in this room today to show a chess board, we would all be able to see how they work together in the whole scheme of things. They do not run along on their own, like pieces were prone to do when some second rate computer or poor amateur player takes over. The Player that we all appreciate can overcome large odds. Often with few pieces he comes out on top. We can all play a doubles match with him! I'm sure that we all have examples of this. Can the audience offer any examples of this happening?

A man in the audience stood up to offer a statement. "The top player made sure that the queen was in the right position to meet this king and they have been a special part of the whole game ever since! My wife and I had three pawns and two have already been promoted! One is now a successful queen in another team!"

JID's father, Nigel, said, "My son is benefiting from a promotion and now has a queen. I'm sure he'll be the winner."

Mark continued, "In the particular game that we are considering, the king and queen are very united, despite being in different parts of the board for a lot of the game so far. All of us can be troubled by opposing knights! They do not move directly, but can be devious when they move. Nothing can get in their way, but the good player knows how to deal with them.

"We are not sure where their castle will be in the in the

immediate future, but they will eventually have the strongest castle of them all!"

The drunken man staggered down the stairs, and fell down the last few, badly spraining his ankle. Oli took him into a spare room where he could be looked after. He went upstairs and quietly spoke to a woman near the back who had First Aid training. She went down to care for him and apply a bandage.

Then flags were removed and Mark carried on with the service. He started by announcing, "I am very happy about the marriage of my daughter to JID. They did not have to ask my permission, but they did and I am happy to give it!"

He continued, "JID and Ruth, I now invite you to join hands and make your vows, in the presence of God and his people."

JID smiled at Ruth, held her hands in front of him and said, "This is the happiest day of my life! I take you as my wife now and for ever. The world has gone crazy, but I am happy to take you for worse, for poorer, in sickness because that is what we are likely to be facing. But God is here and He is the winner!"

Ruth put her arms round JID's waist and pulled him closer. "I could never have expected a man as good as you! Yes, the world is bad, but God is good - and I'm glad that we are facing it together. I take you as my husband in all circumstances, till death us do part."

They had intended to buy a ring, but the jewellers had all been looted of every last trinket. A few days after the transporter disasters, however, it became apparent that even jewellery, the currency in previous times of economic crashes, was going to be valueless. People desperately needed food, so jewellery did not appeal any more. Some kept hold of their jewellery, whether obtained by fair means or foul, in the hope that one day it would have some value again. This situation was so complete and depressing that most people decided that hope, and appreciation of what had been regarded as the finer things of life were pointless. It became common for people to deliberately throw away jewellery, and other items of now pointless trivia. One afternoon JID and Ruth had gone for a walk round Preston and, realising that rings were on the floor for the taking, they tried on scores of rings and held on to any that fitted. After about an hour they checked and found that they both had beautiful, identical rings that fitted perfectly. They would have been expensive rings, but had been rejected as rubbish. To JID and Ruth they were magnificent symbols of a marriage made in Heaven.

Red passed the rings to Mark who prayed the standard prayer of blessing for the rings.

JID took the ring and placed it on her left-hand ring finger. "Ruth, my wonderful wife, I give you this ring as a sign of our marriage. With my body I honour you. I haven't got much now, but I give it all to you, within the love of God, Father, Son and Holy Spirit."

Ruth placed the ring on JID's wedding ring finger and said, "JID, my special husband, I give you this ring as a sign of our marriage. With my body I honour you. I look forward to sharing all we have and are, within the love of God, Father, Son and Holy Spirit."

Mark, with a smile that seemed wider than his face said, "In the presence of God, and before this congregation, JID and Ruth have given their consent and made their marriage vows to each other. They have declared their marriage by the joining of hands and by the giving and receiving of rings. I therefore proclaim that they are husband and wife. God has joined them and nothing can divide them!"

He prayed a prayer of blessing and then various members of the congregation prayed for them. The prayers were joyful, because the people there were overcoming the world around them. They were among the few who had any aim in their lives. They worked like slaves in doing what they could for others, friends and those who chose to be their foes. And they prayed.

The formal part of the proceedings drew to a close about 12 noon and the baptisms followed immediately. The wedding feast started, and what a great feast it was! The food was not what bride, groom and guests would have expected in earlier years, but this feast had even more love and care than anyone could ever have expected!

Some food was provided by the McCallow and Davies families. It had become difficult in the general poverty to provide anything like what would have been expected. Other people brought what they were able to bring. Various people had joined together to make, bake and ice a cake. The amount of food per person was slightly less than they would have had for any ordinary meal before the worst of the recent troubles, but this really was a feast fit for a king (and his new queen!)

The couple received the guests as the guests took it in turns to help to rearrange the furniture for the meal.

The first course was a choice of soups. Oli Timson's shop had been destroyed by a crashing transporter. He had dug for days to rescue any goods that he could, but without very much success. All that he had been able to find was 40 large cans of soup. He hid the soup so that he would be able to survive as long as possible if the situation didn't improve. He had no intention of sharing it with anyone.

After seeing how the Chess Club people had helped him, he was even prepared to give up his soup! He offered the whole lot to the happy couple. There were 80 guests and they were able to have half a can each. He was overjoyed and grateful after the wedding when two people didn't have soup and he got a panful of soup returned to him. He shared it with Ed the next day.

Next came the main course - sandwiches. People had donated yeast, bread flour, cooking fat and other ingredients. There was no electricity or mains gas, but they were able to get a mile or two out of town and created a makeshift oven from wood they cut from the trees. The only recipes they had were destroyed in the disaster, but the loaves that they baked tasted very good, and the circumstances made them taste even better. There was a choice of sandwich fillings.

A family from the Chess Club had been keeping chickens. They were concerned that they were unable to supply enough food for the chickens, so they decided that they would eat some of them. When the wedding was announced they gave five chickens, and did all that was needed to get them ready for the makeshift oven in the countryside.

Another family had stocked up on various sandwich

fillings in tins. Others provided cheese and jam.

After the meal there was fresh fruit from William Howard. He was a Chess Club member who had a large orchard and market garden near the bonfire site. He was able to grow several different kinds of fruit in the low lying rich soil there. He had been at his home in Preston on the day of the disaster, and had been injured by flying masonry. He had been unable to walk very far since then, but he told the others to collect every bit of fruit they could and bring it in for the feast. Various berries were ripe and good to eat. A lot of fruit had already been taken by hungry people, but there was plenty left to make a huge fruit salad, which fed the Wedding Party and many Chess Club members and their guests for weeks. Apples were not yet ripe, but in future months, they would add to the diets of Chess Club members and foragers alike.

Water was scarce and often putrid. Many people had stolen all the alcohol they could find to blot the circumstances out of their mind. The lack of fuel made hot drinks difficult to prepare. Lots of the guests had saved a personal stock of soft drinks, so this may have been the first wedding where the toasts were drunk with lemonade and cola. Speeches followed.

The father of the bride said, "It's good to be able to speak without any suspected unwanted guests! It is wonderful for me to be able to express the joy that we all share in this special marriage. We enjoy and appreciate marriage not because it's the first that most of us have been to for a long time under the cruel social conditions that we have been forced into. It's not because we have been able to have what seems like a miraculous feast in time of severe austerity. It's because we can share the joy of two wise, intelligent and fearless young people. They have seen the way the world has been drifting and, recently, run aground. But they have a faith to swim against the tide and overcome by God's grace. They have a love for each other that will, I am sure, be with them 'as long as they both shall live'. On earth their lives and the lives of all of us may be hanging on a thread, but the person who is faithful to the end WILL be saved!

"As the grateful father of the bride it is my great pleasure to toast the bride and groom."

"The bride and groom!" they all responded.

JID stood to address the party. He started slowly and quietly, "I have been told that these talks usually begin with the words," (he raised his voice slightly) "My wife and I…"

The listeners responded with what had been customary cheering and wisecracking in earlier years.

"We would like to say a big 'Thank you' to lots of people, but first I thank God for all that He gives and makes possible. His son died and rose for us. All life and experience is special when He is with us.

"Thanks to my Dad who made this wedding possible. Even before I met Ruth he recognised that she was a good catch for me! He and my Father-in-Law seemed to have been plotting ruthlessly - or should I say 'Ruthfully!' Thanks to our mothers who have given us both happy homes to imitate. I hope that our home, wherever or however we are able to live in these days, will have the same kind of joy that our parents provided, even if we are unable to have the same comforts that were available in what seems like an earlier age.

"Thank you to Red Young, who showed me that life is not just an aimless drifting in a pointless existence."

"Thanks to all of you for this amazing reception. I would never have imagined that it would be more than a lettuce leaf each! Thank you for coming today, with all the risks involved.

"And thanks to Ruth. I look forward to the greatest human love and togetherness with the most beautiful and intelligent woman I could ever have imagined. Thank you, Ruth.

"My thanks to the bridesmaid and lady-of-honour for looking so beautiful and wearing matching dresses despite the difficulty of arranging them over distances." He didn't know that they had made no effort to be the same. They only discovered that when they arrived. "Let's drink to the magnificent supporters of the bride, Kit and Jane."

"Kit and Jane." The gathering replied.

As the applause died down Ruth stood. "I would like to thank JID for everything. This wedding would not have been possible without him! Everyone has been speaking for too long so I'm not going to! I am deliriously happy with the whole event and I want to add my thanks to JID's.

Red stood up and showed that he had skill as a public speaker as well as a footballer. He started off by thanking the bridesmaid and lady-of-honour, and saying that they had done an excellent job in the way they had looked after and helped Ruth.

He continued his speech in the traditional way by embarrassing the groom. "I first met JID at school. I think it's fair to say that I was quite a good footballer! If people like JID had been as good we would have won a lot more trophies. I often thought that if he could have been sent off instead of me we would have beaten everyone! But you'll be pleased to know that we will not be judged on our football ability when it comes to what matters most! (At least, people like JID will be glad!) JID does not support Merziblu or even Preston. He was a Northampton supporter!" He said the word Northampton with a mock sneering expression. "Still, nobody is perfect! My fixture list tells me that we play Northampton next Saturday at Newison Park. The tickets were printed the day before the disasters, so I have tickets available for half the normal price!

Everyone laughed. They knew that there would be no top football matches in the foreseeable future.

"Ruth and Kit have been friends for many years, and we have made several suggestions about boys who we thought may have fulfilled Ruth's dreams. She never made a quick decision, but, after a few meetings, they all fell short of her expectations.

"The first was too serious so the next we suggested was more lighthearted. He was too silly. The next was too weak so we found one who was almost as strong as me. He was too clumsy. The next was not as bright as her so we found a man with a doctorate. He was too proud of himself.

"Next thing we know she had fallen for a lad who likes *chess!* How can any girl fall for a chess player??? (Perhaps I'd better be careful what I say to members of a chess club!) I met JID, and I found out why she appreciates him! Here is a man who plays chess yet is one of the most thoughtful people I have met. His choice in girls is spot on. If I hadn't met Kit I may well be sitting where JID is now! (No, actually I wouldn't! I would have been too active, or too tall, or too noisy!) JID is able to fit Ruth's exacting standards and I do not think that anyone else could possibly do that!

"We all have our hopes and dreams under severe test these days. Like everyone else, JID and Ruth will have to face the kinds of problems that we would never have met in our worst nightmares even at the start of this year. JID has shown that they can be beaten. I applaud him! May we all stay close to the Lord and, as far as we are able to, as close to each other to tackle the fierce challenges ahead."

The formal part of the reception came to an end and JID danced with Ruth to the music of piano and guitar.

The injured drunkard had been recovering from his hangover and his injury in a room downstairs. When the party started he shyly and very painfully climbed the stairs and went to JID to apologise for his behaviour. JID smiled and welcomed him. He had been overwhelmed by the way that the people at the wedding had looked after him. He had given up hope of ever finding anyone who would treat him sympathetically, like a human being. He had been a drinker for many years, but his drinking was just about under control, until the disasters. After that he had been drinking anything that would go down, including some very suspicious liquids that were really designed as antiseptics or floor cleaners. He said he had had a death wish, and thought that was the way to end it all. He had failed.

Ruth told him to join the party and get some good food down him. He did, but also started to ask people about the reason they were different to everyone else.

There had been no presents other than the food and the presence of the guests - and the happy couple would have it no other way. However, when it was nearly 6pm JID's and Ruth's parents told them that they were going, and that they had a special surprise for them. They were going to walk to Hesketh Bank and stay at Mark's house. They had found a safe route and would cross the bridge over the River Douglas, near their home, when darkness had fallen so that they would not be seen by the self-appointed vigilante groups that were forming everywhere, and were robbing people of anything they regarded as valuable. They would not be carrying anything valuable, as food was the only thing that had any value now.

JID and Ruth tried to dissuade them, but their minds were made up. JID and Ruth would have the luxury of having the house to themselves.

At 7.30pm, JID and Ruth started to walk back to his parents' house. The double bed in the main room had clean sheets and a note, signed by all their parents saying, "Sleep well!!!" They had a drink of lemonade and went to bed early.

. . . . .

The next few weeks were as blissful as the wedding day. JID and Ruth spent a lot of time together and went on occasional walks into the countryside to get food. Of necessity their diet was almost completely vegetarian, with fruit kindly provided by their orchard owner friend, William Howard. One day they had a special treat. William Howard had a friend who kept cattle nearby. They had traded a cow for a similar weight of fruit that morning so JID, Ruth, Red, Kit and a few of their friends went to the orchard to accept the cow and hand over the fruit. They camped in a barn overnight and cooked the whole cow on a bonfire. They sang songs and laughed a lot.

The next day they wrapped and loaded the meat onto handcarts and took it back to Preston in the evening under cover of darkness.

Next morning they took it to William, who was still quite immobile, before he made a list of people to whom he wanted to give meat. They chopped the meat and went around the area delivering it. That took all day for a team of about ten people. They were unable to carry or cart large amounts in daylight or they would have been seen as fair game by vigilantes. If they went in a group they would risk being dragged into gang warfare, so they went out in ones and twos with small loads.

The visits were joyful events as they caught up with the others from the Chess Club. In turn the people who received the meat were overwhelmed - most were not sure where the next meal would come from. They hung around chatting for half an hour or more in each house so that they would not draw attention to themselves if they seemed to be involved in some organised activity.

· · · · ·

After two weeks JID's parents returned from Hesketh Bank. JID and Ruth were delighted that they had survived and looked so well, despite (or perhaps because) they were slightly thinner than before. The house was, of course, much more crowded, but they fitted in and cooperated in the complicated tasks of daily life.

# Chapter 8. August.
# The Loss of the Leaders...

'Archbishop' Joe King clicked his fingers and the waitress brought him a fourth hamburger with barbecue sauce. He put an arm around her waist and pulled her towards him. The waitress playfully gave Joe a peck on the cheek then deftly stepped aside and away from him. Jean Brett, Oscar Victor and a few hangers on at the table giggled and gave a drunken cheer. They were enjoying the tropical evening sun by the hotel pool as they had for the last month or so. Joe's wife knew that the only way she could enjoy the luxury lifestyle was to patiently put up with his antics.

In the 18th and 19th centuries discredited rulers in Western Europe had had a reliable escape route. They would go to any other country they had not recently been at war with and be treated well. The rulers of that country would have no problem in accepting them provided they did not use their asylum home as a base for questionable political activity. The reason that the host nation's rulers accepted them was that, when their own turn came to flee, other countries accepted them. The old-boys' network was alive and well, and won every time! That system worked for a long time until radio and telephone began to develop, the misdeeds of bad rulers became more generally known and political asylum became much less common and harder to win.

Now in the 21$^{st}$ century, of course, rulers still had the same desire and instinct for self-preservation. They had much more power than ever before, but the rulers still realised that even with their immense power, or perhaps because of it, their lives could be in danger. The way the Western rulers planned their getaway was to take over the Cape Verde Island of Sao Lucia. It was about 15 kilometres long. In the distant past it had been a green and pleasant land, but the black rocks had been exposed and the island had become a desert. While other Cape Verde Islands became tourist hotspots, Sao Lucia was largely abandoned. That made it a perfect place for the heaven-on-earth that the rulers planned for themselves. The Government of Iberia had moved in. Other Governments also poured their population's money into the scheme. Military barracks were placed on the East coast so their armies would be able to protect the VIPs, while the rest of the island was the playground and potential exile home of those with the most power and money. There were rumours, probably true, that tactical nuclear weapons were stationed there to deter any unwelcome interference.

Very soon the black island became green again, this time by a huge investment in water pumping and land management. The soil was very fertile and soon there were farms producing crops and animals. A small airport was built (the only airport newly built for a decade). This was followed by hotels and other attractions to the South East of the army base. The population in other nearby islands had their own tourist and hospitality industry. Selected people were recruited and were well paid to look after a comparatively small number of guests from the upper crust of various societies. Most of these facilities remained in this strange state of existence for a while after they were developed. They were capable of comfortably housing about 3,000 guests in ten luxury hotels, but ran almost empty despite the fact that the staff were paid their full salary to be there and ready to work.

Huge banks of solar energy panels facing almost vertically turned equatorial sunrays into all the electric power that would ever be needed. This powered, among other things, freezers and refrigerators, which stored a year's supply of provisions for full hotels.

When monsoon rains hit the island, holidaymaking bosses could enjoy the protection from rain and ultraviolet by various anticlimate umbrella domes, which looked similar to the ones developed for the

Eden Project in Cornwall. Top people often had holidays there, but they knew that one day political or environmental conditions may necessitate moving permanently to Sao Lucia. When the gravity-reversal system failed, that day arrived. If they stayed put, at best they would suffer with the rest of the population. At worst they would be found and made to suffer much more at the hands of the inevitable, and now very real, vigilantes.

Aircraft were history - except for the private jets that the power classes kept in museums like Heathrow. None had flown since the coming of gravity-reversal. The new transporters had been able to fly and stop themselves colliding with each other, but there was never any way they could avoid collisions with conventional aircraft, so conventional aircraft were banned for ever. Unless an extraordinary need arose...

It arose as soon as the Gravity-reversal transporters collapsed. People with money and power knew that their safety depended on getting well away from Northwesteurope - and every other country where they lived- as quickly as possible. The drives of their homes were deliberately built long enough for them and their families to take off in microlights. They flew to Heathrow or other centres where there were mothballed aircraft. They were then whisked to Sao Lucia.

. . . . .

Joe King had eaten well earlier in the evening, and he was now coming to the end of his time on the stage. As always, his quick fire humour often had the audience in hysterics. He came to the end of his penultimate joke, and he quickly went back to the end of an unfinished joke from earlier. "You remember the story of the nurse in the abattoir? She went out and shouted, 'Maybe, but I'm not French!'

The audience fell about laughing. Joe King remained a great star.

. . . . .

The megacompanies trailblazers had met in strictly secret conditions two years earlier to decide who they would invite to be on the evacuation list. The only people allowed on Sao Lucia (apart from selected politicians and industrialists) were the ones who looked after them. While the bosses realised that the Worldfaith leaders had served them well, they were expendable if the worst came to the worst and excluded from the list, so Joe King's service to companies did not save him. He was only put on the Sao Lucia list when one of the power men nominated him as an entertainer. He had never failed to capture an audience, and wondered why the leaders of traditional Christianity turned against him. He had tried everything from twisted argument to emotional appeals and accusations.

Top broadcasters and news reporters were also among the ones who were kept alive on Sao Lucia. At some future date the megacompanies may be able to use them and their skills. It was impossible for anyone to foresee what would come next, but the greatest minds in the megacompanies were trying to understand what might be next and how they could exploit the imaginary situation. Could they, for instance, take over other islands and, over a period of years, take parts of Africa. Dakar, the capital of Eastern Sahara was about 800 kilometres away and would be their first target.

They always failed to see the significance of the wider situation. Neither could Gaucho Gonzales, but that did not stop him from seizing the immediate situation to his own advantage! He often travelled the world for his latest adventures, but when Gravity-reversal failed he was in Terminal 4, which he now regarded as his home. He saw a few small planes take off soon after the disaster, and knew exactly what was happening. His spies in the companies had kept him informed of Sao Lucia being developed as the ultimate bolthole for megacompany leaders. He knew that the collapse of gravity-reversal would, sooner or later, be inevitable. He also knew that Terminal 4 would be one of the few places in Northwesteurope that would be safe when they fell from the sky. Transporters didn't fly too near to Heathrow so that their collapse would not damage the bosses' escape runways, and so that it would be more difficult for Gonzales to shoot any transporters down at any stage.

Gonzales was no fool. His men could have shot down any conventional plane they aimed at, and a lot of them asked for permission to do just that when the refugee planes left. He refused because he had greater plans.

Five weeks later he sent six launches, each holding 25 commandos, to the North end of Sao Lucia. They arrived at night and hid a couple of bays away from the military garrison. Ten men were sent on a raiding party. They knew exactly where the commander-in-chief of the garrison would be that night, having a party with the other top officers. The raiding party's job was to surround the base and 'neutralise' any guards who appeared. (None did, they had such huge confidence in their own security and thought that nobody would bother attacking them.) Next came the attack. A light flashed as a signal to start the countdown. On 'zero', ten rocket-propelled grenades simultaneously flew to the sports hall where the officers were feasting. The rockets flattened the sports hall and everyone in it.

The other men in the garrison had no idea what to do next. Some got into defensive positions ready for whatever attack followed. Others realised that they had no chain of command and that every man was for himself. They ran in every direction from the camp and into the grasp of the commandos. The commandos could see them, but they could not see the commandos. When the commandos gave orders for them to throw away their weapons and lie face down, most did. A few of them decided to aim in the direction of the voices, but had no chance in the darkness against unseen men with night vision goggles.

By the morning, 130 men (almost a quarter of the garrison) had been captured by the commandos. Meanwhile, Gonzales and the rest of his force had crossed ten kilometres of rough land and reached the mountain overlooking the garrison camp. He had the prisoners of war sat in rows in front of him and addressed them.

"Fellow soldiers, I salute you." He announced in a loud voice, followed by a very formal salute and smile in their direction, slowly turning to right and left to face them all in turn. "I always appreciate the bravery of elite fighting men like yourselves. But you must always remember that no fighting force can be better than their leadership, and the leadership you have had was the worst! They didn't take any precautions against the possibility of invasion. They didn't even have lookouts around the camp. They had a false sense of security and thought that nobody would attempt to attack. I, Gaucho Gonzales proved them wrong.

At the mention of his name several of the garrison men looked terrified. His fierce, uncompromising reputation would always strike fear into the hearts of military and civilians alike all round the world. However, they needn't have worried - they were a part of Gonzales' plan.

"Yes, you miserable dogs are right to fear me, but we can strike a deal. If you and the people in the camp decide to join my cause I will give you *proper* training, a pay rise and a more thrilling lifestyle than you would ever get serving a bunch of overfed buffoons who want to treat you with the contempt they show to the rest of the world. What do you think?"

The captives did not know what to make of Gonzales and his offer. Could he be trusted? And was there really any choice?

"Well? What do you say?" roared Gonzales. "Can you give me an answer? Or maybe you want to ask some questions?"

With fear and trembling one man, put a hand up. Ten rifles pointed at him. "Don't shoot unless I say so," shouted Gonzales. "Now you," he said, pointing to the man, "Stand up. I admire your courage. What was your rank and name?"

"Sergeant Louis Noir, Sir." He replied.

"Then speak, sergeant."

"Can we ask what you have in mind? Do you want to overcome the company men or team up with them? If we join your force how will we fit into your plans? What is the alternative? Why should we fight for you rather than against you?" He realised that his questions were dangerous for him, personally, but he wanted to find out more about what he was dealing with, and get time for himself and others to figure out some way of delaying the work of Gonzales if they thought that he may be turning against them in any way.

"Hey, a thinker!" shouted Gonzales. "I need thinkers. I promote you. Sergeant, you are now sergeant major!" He signalled to one of his soldiers who took a bright green ribbon from the rucksack on the back of another. The man put the ribbon round the neck of the promoted prisoner and shook his hand. "My plan will be to become the head of this force of yours. Anyone who chooses to fight against me will be instantly terminated, but if you are on my side I will be on yours! I would not advise anyone to defy me. My force is just 150 men in all. You see how ten of us arrested all of you! We have enough fire power to demolish your whole garrison in minutes.

"The aim is to force the companies' leaders to be sorry for their previous actions. They will finally be shown the folly of working against the people! I could have brought a force 20 times this size to take over this island, with a lot of unnecessary bloodshed, but I'd rather deal with hearts and minds! In this case *your* hearts and minds. Decision time is approaching! I need to know if you are with me or against me! But I'm not going to leave the decision to you! I want you to go back into the camp and talk to the others. If you come out of the camp unarmed I will meet you and the training will commence. Which of you has the highest rank here?

"I am sergeant major Grau!" said one man.

"I promote you to sergeant!" said Gonzales, to the joy and amusement of his own men and the prisoners alike. "Are there any other sergeants?"

Six put up their hands. They and the former sergeant major were issued with blue ribbons. The rest received red ribbons.

"Now get up and go to the camp," Gonzales said to the leaders. "At 2pm you must all come out of the camp unarmed and with your hands up. Any resistance will be crushed. Put the men in the camp in the picture. They will not regret joining me! They *will* regret opposing me! And remember that the people to the south-west must not know about the change of Government yet! I would like to surprise them myself!

. . . . .

It was approaching 10am and the bosses were getting up at their normal breakfast time in the hotels. They were trying to decide if it would be worth trying to get some idea of the state of the world but they had various problems. They had no way of knowing how to get any information from anywhere else. They would find transport difficult. They would need spies to do their work because, if any of them appeared, they would run too much risk of assassination.

Like most of their decisions they decided to face the question at another meeting as there was no hurry. If they were short of means of transport then it was certain that everyone else was even worse off. Would they spend their natural lives living in unnatural luxury and unaccustomed laziness? While the thought may have been appealing in the short term the former high-flyers knew that a lack of challenge would eventually lead to lack of any motivation and aim. Some decided to specialise in farming, so that when the food stocks ran out they would be able to apply their minds to producing the food for the future and becoming the next generation of leaders. That idea seemed good to the bosses, but they then came up against the Verdean farmers who were already tending the farms for them. The Verdeans knew how to farm that kind of countryside and climate well. They weren't for sharing their information with the bosses or anyone else. The bosses thought of giving serious punishment to the farmers, perhaps even shooting a few, but they then decided that they would not get any others to help on Sao Lucia, and while they developed the required knowledge they would suffer severe hunger and poverty. They considered the situation and decided that 'if it's not broke we won't fix it.'

The one who had the responsibility of coordinating with the local garrison reported that he had not been able to have the customary talk with the garrison commander that morning, but it was probably a bug in the machinery. The army would be able to sort that out for them. Everyone else nodded and they went on to the next point, which had been deferred three days earlier.

At 11am that day they planned to have their daily water polo match. They had kept changing the make-up of the teams and they now had six teams that were very closely matched. At about noon most went to the nearby beach. They swam and then sunbathed - while the less energetic just sunbathed.

After the midday meal they would have a well-earned siesta and most would play or watch tennis. In the evening it was snooker followed by supper, then Joe King and a 2000-2009 revival pop group, The Noughties, consisting of several members of the top groups of that period.

. . . . .

That had become the usual pattern of events. Every day was the same as the last one and, while each person was convinced of his own mental well-being, each saw worrying signs in the others. The real problem was extreme boredom - a condition that had not affected any of them while they plotted and schemed in their home nations where they had absolute power, but also had a lot to do.

Every day was exactly the same as the last one - until the day that Gaucho Gonzales decided it was time to change.

. . . . .

Most of the soldiers of the Sao Lucia garrison appeared at 2pm, unarmed, with their hands up walking from their barracks. Some decided to be heroes and fight. Shots rang out from between buildings and two of the men who had surrendered fell. Simultaneously there were shots from some of the other buildings towards Gonzales' men. Gonzales shouted an order to the ones who were surrendering, telling them to lie on the ground, so that he and his men would be able to have a clear view of the buildings. After about ten minutes of fighting the barracks went quiet. Gonzales ordered his new sergeant major, Louis Noir to come to collect arms, then organise a search of the buildings to see if there were any further rebels. He hand-picked a dozen or so men to do a search with him. A few minutes into the search of the extensive buildings there was a gunfight that lasted for less than a minute. His men survived the gunfights, but two were killed when a booby trap bomb exploded.

Half an hour later they had completed the search of the extensive camp. They returned to the open area near the camp entrance and called to Gonzales that it was all clear.

Gonzales ordered his own lieutenants to go into the camp, with Noir to show them around. They took control of all the weapons so that they could test the loyalty of the former company troops before they allowed them to have weapons.

Gonzales asked who was in charge of communications. The man, known as 'Ham', had been the one who maintained the link with the leading bosses. Gonzales told Ham to continue the broadcasts. He said that he had tapped into the messages for the last fortnight and would recognise any attempt to send coded messages. This was, as Ham suspected, complete lies. However, there was no agreed code with the bosses and even if there was, Ham would take no chances.

For the next few days Gonzales socialised with the former company men and got them on his side the way he had done so often and (usually) so effectively at his headquarters in Peru in earlier days.

Gonzales' lessons in tactics included a detailed series of lectures on the tactical mistakes that had been made by their former leaders. They arranged for lookouts to surround the camp 24/7. The lookouts would be in touch with each other throughout their time of duty to defend against a counterattack by megacompany forces or betrayal by other lookouts. Gonzales was very 'hands- on' as a leader, and he encouraged all his officers to be the same. Noir and his sergeants all took their share in every duty including the guard duty.

His lessons to the newer men included details of how the chain of command worked in his organisation. Although he took his share in guard duty and every other job, including cooking and cleaning the latrines, he was, and would always be, the extreme commander. Before any planned action he would discuss it with the men and they would be welcome to express their hopes, fears and ideas. Often he would amend plans to include the wisdom of his men. But when they were involved in any action, planned or emergency, they must obey commands without question. The soldiers would have to use initiative where necessary, but always within the commands from superior officers.

The men were all issued with new uniforms and were told to put aside their company uniforms to save as souvenirs. The new uniforms had a special type of reflective surface, which reflected the colour of the ground roughly horizontally. When used on sand they appeared brown. Over grass they seemed green.

Gonzales arranged four training exercises, but the men knew that they would not be allowed to use live ammunition until Gonzales accepted their loyalty. After the third he announced that they would attack the bosses' hotels in the next few weeks, but that he would not tell them until it was imminent, for security reasons. The last exercise would be the following week.

. . . . .

Two nights later a group of soldiers broke out of the camp and shot a lookout. The emergency plan swung into action. As soon as the shot was heard the lookouts tried to contact each other and sent a report to Gonzales' lieutenant. He tannoyed the entire camp, asking if all were present.

"Barrack 1." "All present", came the reply.

"Barrack 2." "All present".

"Barrack 3." "All present",

"Barrack 4." "All present except for those on guard duty".

"Gonzales force barrack 1." There was silence.

"GF1, respond immediately." Still silence.

"Gonzales force barrack 2." "All present."

"Gonzales force barrack 3." "All present."

Gonzales sounded concerned, but in control. "We have a serious emergency!" he roared. "It seems that we have had a mutiny my friends. I have tested the loyalty of the former Garrison Force so I am going to have to rely on my new men. Gonzales forces take your arms and protect the camp perimeter while arms are issued to our new friends. If you see any of the GF1 men, shoot on sight. All men get your uniforms and night vision equipment on and report to the parade ground.

Within three minutes, all of the remaining forces arrived at the parade ground. They didn't form into formal lines (they had been drilled by Gonzales not to - it was much more important to stay alert and look out in all directions.) Each man was provided with a purple ribbon to prove which side he was on, and with a high-powered rifle with telescopic sights. Gonzales said, "We need to wipe out the opposition. Show no mercy. You all carry a purple ribbon but the rebels do not. Anybody you see without the ribbon is an essential target and must be killed. I will lead the group going inland to the east. Noir will lead his group south-eastwards. Grau is his second in command. My lieutenant will lead the northward group. We have the opportunity to start a new chapter in military history! Today, Sao Lucia, soon the whole island. In a short time you will join with the rest of my force to conquer the world!

"These guns fire a new kind of bullet. They are designed to leave the rifle at a comparatively slow speed and are then accelerated by a rocket system within the bullet. The advantage is that they produce a minimum of kickback and you can aim better. I am so confident of the teamwork we have that garrison men and my original team are in each group. To your posts and towards victory!!

As they started to get into their groups to leave, one of the men from Gonzales' original force, who was still thought to be loyal to Gonzales, turned his rifle towards Gonzales and aimed a shot. Another one of Gonzales' force was unfortunate enough to get in the way of the bullet and fell. Immediately, several men, garrison men and Gonzales' men all shot at the one who had shot at Gonzales. He fell down groaning. Gonzales called to the medical branch, "Keep this swine alive. I want to deal with him personally." He then shouted, "Towards the victory," And the men went out towards their enemy. The medics came out with stretchers and looked after the men who had been shot.

As expected, the task was not easy. The rebels were well hidden and were ready for the force to approach. They approached as warily as possible. The three groups kept in touch by old style field radios, all the commanders could hear all that each other said. About three hours into the operation the eastward group, led by Gonzales, spotted a lookout for the rebels. Gonzales told them not to draw attention by shooting until they were told. He sent a message to the northward and southward groups giving the coordinates.

Eventually they figured out that they were on four peaks approximately in a square about three or four kilometres between each peak. Gonzales told the commanders that they would describe the peaks as A, B, C and D, and carefully said which was which.

When each group reached the area they sent a message to Gonzales. Gonzales told each group to reccy the area and send any information they had to each other because the better informed they were, the better chance they had of achieving the objective. They all knew that in this kind of situation the defenders who were dug in would probably have all the advantages and, although the defenders would lose against a much greater force, the attackers would be likely to suffer very heavy injuries and fatalities. The men gritted their teeth for what would be a difficult operation.

On a given signal the attackers started firing together. The first bullets were carefully aimed at the lookouts.

The operation had been so well carried out so far that the rebels had no idea that the attack was imminent. As the sentries fell, shots rang out from the four peaks that overlooked the area. The attackers knew that the rest of the operation would be a bitter battle. They were under fire as they inched up the tricky steep lava slopes. The lava crumbled under the weight of boots and each two steps forward led to one slide backwards. They did their best, looking for whatever cover they could find. There was some rough grass on the slopes that held the lava together and helped them to climb, but the trees and bushes that had been planted to improve the appearance of the island had not grown enough to provide cover or protection.

Gunfire was deafening as the attackers marched onwards. Some fell, but others were able to continue the attack, occasionally picking off a defender.

Gonzales and his commanders had all the hand grenades and used them to good effect several times. When hills A and C were conquered, the surviving attackers from those forces joined to attack hill D.

As soon as the firing started at Hill D, Grau decided to use the confusion to settle a score. He aimed at Noir and pulled the trigger twice. The rifle's mechanism jammed. He swore, hid and tried to adjust his rifle. He found that he was unable to make any adjustment, but, as he tried to see what the problem was, he accidentally pressed the trigger and a shot rang out sending a bullet into the early morning air. He continued fighting uphill, until he got close enough to pick out Noir. He shot, and this time Noir fell face down and slid a few metres down the hill. Grau smiled and then continued to join the advance.

When the firing was at its loudest, and men on every side were keeping as low as possible, Gonzales stood up and started walking towards the defenders. The men with him shouted to warn him and get him to take cover. He then pressed a switch and every rifle went quiet. He pulled a microphone from his pocket and his voice rang out from huge speakers at the top of hills B and D! "All right men, exercise over!"

The men who had been defending the hill, including Noir and all the others who had been shot, apparently dead stood up and walked towards Gonzales. It turned out that the attackers who had fallen (apart from Noir) were all members of the original Gonzales team. They also stood up and joined the others. "Back to the camp", shouted Gonzales.

On the way back to the camp they met men of both sides who had been 'fighting' on Hill B. When they arrived at the camp the medics (and the men who had been 'shot' before the operation) had prepared a huge meal for everyone. When most of the men had finished their dessert Gonzales stood up. "It's my birthday!" He shouted. The garrison men had been told about the phrase, and joined in with the cheering and rhythmical clapping.

"As so often in battle, some men were trying to settle personal scores. It would be wonderful for a commander to know just who these men were, but how can we know?" At this, Grau and some others who thought that they may have been caught out visibly relaxed.

"As is customary, on my birthday I am the one who gives gifts! Every man here will be given a 10% payrise!!" All cheered, but some realised that money had little meaning now.

He continued, "We can learn a lot about future tactics from the experience of this kind of operation, where the entire force, except for a few trusted men, think that they are in a real battle. We can see who are the brave men, who are the cowards and who are the traitors. I did not see any treachery, but I saw a lot of good practise, and I want to commend those who did extreme acts of heroism. When I call your name, come forward.

He called four names and the men came forward. Three were from the garrison. "These men helped the attackers on Hill A by keeping the defenders busy and making room for others to make a lot of headway." He then shouted "Pictures!" A map of that part of the island was projected onto every wall. It showed the position of every man. On the maps, attackers were red dots, defenders were in blue and the four men standing at the front were in white on the screen. It showed the 'white' men surrounding the defenders and shooting from close range while the other attackers found another way up to the defenders position and picked them off. "These men are heroes!" said Gonzales.

He called out six names of men on hill D. Again he showed the map which looked like a computer game. Again he said why the men were distinguished and described them as heroes. This went on for about half an hour.

He then said "And now will sergeant Grau come forward."

Grau got to his feet, but was not sure why he had been called. Had his plan been spotted? "Come forward my friend," said Gonzales. "Sit down here and we will see what makes you a hero. What you did not know was that every rifle had a small 3Dvid camera! Nothing has been missed. Let's see what you achieved.

Grau was worried, but soon began to relax again. "We needed reinforcements for the men near the top of Hill D." said Gonzales. "Grau had been delayed at the lower levels, but I want you to see how he added to the effective power of the group. He is the yellow dot on this screen. He was under fire yet acted without concern for his own safety."

Grau remembered the incident, but at the time he was temporally unaware of the strength of the defenders there. He was furious that Noir had escaped his earlier attempt on his life.

"Despite tackling a gradient of over 35%, on terrain that slips so easily and can take lives even when there is no gunfire, Grau was undaunted. Watch this picture in real time."

While the dots were moving slowly up the hill, and each one was picking his way forward slowly trying to remain under cover, Grau's dot started to accelerate. He made about a 100 metres horizontally and 20 vertically in about 20 seconds.

They then projected pictures from Grau's rifle, from just after the initial shots aimed at Noir until just before his later shot 'hit' Noir. He was very relieved that the earlier and later pictures had, amazingly, been missed by the analysts.

"Please applaud Grau!" On Gonzales' suggestion every man rose to his feet and clapped. Grau breathed a sigh of relief and got to his feet to return to his seat when Gonzales said, "What is the hurry! Stay and talk with me."

Gonzales sat down and the other men stayed put, chatting about the operation and the part they all played. Gonzales talked with Grau and asked details of his life, family, aims and other trivia. Gonzales then stood up again and addressed the whole assembly. When the talking died down he said, "I have told you some of the story of Grau, but now let me continue. I will now show you the whole story!"

The screens showed the scene from Grau's rifle from a few seconds before the fighting started. The audience heard the sound of shots all around, and the view from the rifle was fast moving and confused. Then the view of Noir's back stayed in view, and the picture flashed twice when Grau pressed the trigger, but Noir was unharmed.

Grau realised that he was in serious trouble, and decided that his only option was to alert the megacompany bosses and get them on his side. He glanced round the room and saw that he was about five metres from the nearest door. While everyone else was seeing the view from his rifle he made a dash for the door. The door swung open and Noir, who had been behind the door, put a bullet into Grau's foot. Two men grabbed hold of Grau and he was chained to a chair.

"I'm sorry, it seems that Mr. Grau missed part of the film he was starring in!" said Gonzales. "Perhaps we can start it again for his benefit." The teleclip started again and Grau was forced to watch. It showed his three attempts to kill Noir, who had been promoted over his head.

"If only Grau had had the bravery to speak when invited, maybe he would have remained as lieutenant. But perhaps not, because even before then my intelligence group told me that he managed to be deeply unpopular with his men. We don't need scum like him in our organisation. We will deal with him later!"

As Grau sat there terrified and in pain, seven other men who had turned against others were indicted, and the evidence was shown. They too were chained to chairs.

Then six men were similarly accused, this time of cowardice. They were shot immediately their names were called.

"Right men, you know the drill. I need the toilet!" said Gonzales as he left the room. The garrison men did not know the drill, but soon found out and joined in enthusiastically against the traitors.

. . . . .

Gonzales was now convinced that he had men who would be willing and able to do or die for him and his questionable ideals. He had a complete list of the bosses he would like to capture with the outside possibility that he may be able to get some ransom money or favours at a later date. He put Joe King on the ransom list for the same reason that the bosses had taken him, not for value, but for humour.

Three days after the selection campaign, the operation against the bosses started and quickly finished. It was quick, simple and effective. Gonzales' men were waiting for darkness in the hills round the hotels. Two men broke into each of the eight power substations that served the hotels. At midnight on the dot they switched off all the power. Most guests were already in their rooms, but the ones at the pool or in the bars were the first to be dealt with. Joe King and eight of the 20 potential hostages were arrested at the pool. Seventeen other people near the pool were shot and killed. Similar operations took place at the other hotels.

They then broke into the hotel rooms and dealt with the inhabitants. Some tried fighting and a few had weapons in their hands, but they were no match for hardened soldiers. When a hostage was taken the name was reported to Gonzales and another man who kept the score. All the hostages were soon taken. They were, as expected, on the VIP floor of the Excelsior Hotel, which was the first place Gonzales' men looked. When the last hostage was captured the message was sent to the division commanders, who evacuated the hotels. When the last man was out of each hotel, the large artillery was brought in to demolish the hotel and make sure that there was nobody left to tell the tale. The Excelsior Hotel was saved from demolition and became the new headquarters for Gonzales, as he planned the next step.

# Chapter 9. September.
# The Outsiders come inside...

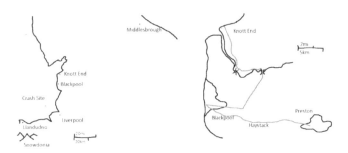

Every step was painful for the man. He and his girlfriend had started the journey in Llandudno, North Wales, and they had decided to stay there that night to appreciate the magnificent views of the mountains of Snowdonia. They had been on a sightseeing transporter and were able to see views that seemed even more impressive than they did from the ground as the changing evening light illuminated the breathtaking scenery.

He had been addressing a large group of people who were all listening carefully and taking in every word. They had become big favourites in their field and they attracted big audiences, although not everyone appreciated him. She was handing out leaflets and answering general questions from the admiring group after his lectures from the podium. The next morning they boarded the transporter for their next venue, Middlesbrough.

That was the morning that the transporters fell from the sky. They thought they would be killed when their transporter started the descent. People and furniture took off in the temporary zero gravity situation, before the expected sickening crash. Everyone in the transporter, however, survived the initial crash because it landed in the sea. The impact, heavy as it was, did not crush the transporter and the impact was much less violent than if the transporter had hit land or anything solid. Most, like billions of others worldwide, expected that the emergency services would soon send transportivances to the rescue. When that didn't happen after several hours they had begun to panic. Many started to swim expecting the transporter to sink, but they were soon carried away by the strong currents and died of exposure.

He and she had always been capable, inventive people. Like everyone else on board the floating hulk, they spent their time thinking the 'what- ifs'. They looked at everything on the transporter to see if it could somehow be used to attract attention, to navigate to the shoreline that they could see far off to the east, or even to eat.

After three days without food they decided it was time to go. He had broken into the energy module and decided to put a lot of the cable to what was now a better use. He had pulled out several lengths of cable all over three metres long. He took hold of another and pulled it out as usual, but as he took the other end somehow the apparently dead machine gave him an electric shock, which did him no real harm, but seriously shook him. He swore, took a few minutes to recover and completed the job.

The vital part of his scheme depended on the mock leather cushions of the seats being waterproof. They looked waterproof. They floated as if they were waterproof. But would they be waterproof long enough to get the couple to land? They didn't know, but they were determined to try as they could see no real alterative.

They took four cushions, each two metres long, and tied them by the metal frames at the back, which had held them to the chairs before he had smashed them off. He put two on top and two underneath, forming a precarious square platform about two metres by two.

Other people had taken an interest. He told them to watch the whole operation carefully before starting to make their own rafts. He told them of the many similar cable lengths in the energy module, and talked of the way to tie them. They had also broken off some of the arms of settees to use as oars and told the 'audience' about it.

When they were ready they set off paddling as if their lives depended on getting as far away from the transporter as they possibly could. That was because their lives DID depend on getting as far away from the transporter as they possibly could. The other passengers would soon find out that they had taken ALL of the cable from the energy module. If there were a couple of good swimmers on board they would be able to catch their raft. Although he and she would have all the advantages in a fight with people trying to board from the sea, they didn't want that fight to happen as they had not eaten for several days and were feeling very weak.

That day the weather was very warm, and they paddled as best they could using the sofa arms. They then realised that they could move the raft quicker by lying on their stomachs and doing the breast stroke kick in the water. They had no idea how far they would have to move the raft or how long it would take. By early evening they were exhausted and tried to get comfortable. They had wanted to stay awake if they could as they would be in danger of falling off the raft if they fell asleep. They held hands for affection and comfort, but mainly so that, if either did fall off, the other would know and be able to come to the rescue.

That night they both drifted in and out of consciousness, but there was no disaster for them. The raft sagged in the middle and they were both kept in by good, old-fashioned gravity although they did get wet. They desperately needed that sleep. It was next morning, they had no idea what time it was, when they were woken suddenly. The gentle swaying of the raft was replaced by a sudden jolt. They both woke up and quickly took in the situation. They had hit land.

Between coughs and splutters they gave the nearest thing they could to a cheer. They climbed out on to mud and walked a few paces to a drier spot. A hundred metres away they could see a bungalow and went for help. They could see the wreckage of five transporters from where they were. When they got to the bungalow they tried to attract the attention of the inhabitants, but nobody answered. They climbed in through a window and looked around. The bungalow had not been used for several days. There was no power and there was the smell of sour milk coming from the fridge. They found some biscuits, some bottles of Timbros and cans of soft drinks. They rapidly devoured the biscuits and whatever they found that was still edible. After a cold shower (with the little water that was in the reservoir in the loft) they got dried and collapsed naked under plenty of blankets to a deep, warm sleep.

Next morning they felt stronger. They looked round the bungalow and salvaged anything that may come in useful. They hadn't yet taken in the full effect of the disaster, but they had already gathered that it had had a much greater effect than just causing their own transporter to crash. They tried to find out more and automatically switched on the 3Dvid. Of course, it, like everything else, was powerless.

They looked around and wondered why they had failed to see Blackpool Tower when they climbed ashore. The Tower, looming almost 200 metres above Blackpool Promenade was some distance to the south of them.

They realised that the people they knew and worked with were far to the south and they started to walk. They decided to stop at Blackpool and find themselves a boarding house for a few days so that they would be able to get stronger and assess the situation.

That was a serious mistake although any decision they made would have had serious drawbacks.

They had landed near Knott End and followed the coast towards Blackpool. After ten kilometres of walking they met the estuary of the River Wyre. They followed the river to find a crossing point, but were unable to do so that day. They saw what looked like a crossing, but as they got closer the truth dawned on them. A small transporter had demolished it. They couldn't safely cross the river. They were exhausted and decided to shelter under a ruined, but sturdy, piece of bridge. That would keep them dry and out of the wind if the weather turned against them. They slept solidly for eight hours and could have slept longer, but they were woken by water. This was not rain but the tide coming in.

He sensed the water before she did, so he woke her urgently and they rescued what they could of their baggage, which consisted of some clothing and food salvaged from the bungalow. Some food was damaged, but most was tinned food and survived the wetting. Shivering violently, they shared a cold tin of baked beans with sausage and set off (slower than the previous day in their wet clothes) to find another river crossing. After another day's hike of 12 kilometres through muddy fields they found the next bridge and were glad to be able to put the River Wyre behind them. After yet another day's walk they got to the other side of the bridge they had reached 48 hours earlier. They camped for the night in the remains of a haystack and felt warmer than they had for days, before breakfasting on a tin of sardines and marching along the old roads towards the outskirts of Blackpool. As soon as they got near the town a group of vigilantes tackled and beat them up before taking their packs. They staggered to their feet and walked on. They reached the hundreds of hotels stretching along the Promenade and fully expected that some were still in operation. Even the few that were running just before the disasters had now closed. Some were demolished. Blackpool Tower was still standing, but part of the Tower Buildings below had been damaged.

He had suffered much worse than she in the attack and a couple of hours later he could take no more, and he collapsed. A couple saw her from their home (formerly a boarding house) and came to the rescue. They carried him into the house, gave them both clean clothes and let them have a bath. The water was not what they would have expected from a Blackpool boarding house in earlier days. Jim and Jane, their hosts, had carried several buckets of water from the beach across the road from their home earlier in the day.

They introduced themselves as Fred and Julia Crompton.

Jane, the landlady, explained that she had often complained about Jim's habit of stocking up with food, bottled water, clothes or anything else of value.

"I bet you're glad now!" he interrupted. "My idea was to have enough goodies at home to last us two years in case of civil breakdown and we were approaching that target. If we are on our own we will be able to last for 19 months. We have been keeping our heads down and not letting anyone see us if we can help it. We go to the beach each day for water to wash in and to stretch our legs, but we go under cover of darkness.

Jane then said, "We love each other very much, but we were beginning to get on each other's nerves. When we saw you we realised you were not part of a gang and felt sorry for you.

Jane said that it was time for tea and disappeared into the kitchen. After an hour Jane came out with a magnificent meal, made even sweeter by their circumstances. It was a tender lamb stew complete with potatoes, onions and beans. This was followed down by a choice of fruit cocktail or rice pudding. After eating they had a choice of Timbros, gin, various wines or soft drinks.

Each day Jim spent a couple of hours on an exercise bike, which was connected to a generator. He had bought the bike on the internet a few years earlier. Again he did it 'in case of civil breakdown'. Because of his obsession they were able to have a nearly normal life. That evening, however, Fred upset Jim and nearly caused a fist fight by putting a light on. "What do you think you are doing?" shouted Jim, knocking Fred over as he dived for the switch and turned the light off.

He asked Jim what the problem was. "The problem," stressed Jim, trying to keep calm "is that if the morons out there know how we live here they will make sure we will not be able to in future."

Fred asked Jim and Jane to explain further. They explained that in the short time since the disasters, even the calmest person would batter their parents if they thought that they could get more food or basic comforts.

After two days Jim and Jane told Fred and Julia that they could stay as long they wished as they enjoyed their company. Jim and Jane were tremendous people, but Fred and Jane had been the kind who would be likely to batter their own parents even before the disaster, but they would not do a thing to harm their kind, naïve hosts. They fitted in well at Jim and Jane's home. She helped with the cooking and he generated their share of the electricity. At the table they faced the wall with the crucifix on it, and thought it was a waste of space and too macabre for today. They mentioned the crucifix and said that it was strange that people still worshipped things like that. Jim smiled and said that they didn't worship the crucifix! It helped them remember what Jesus did for people who follow him. They nodded politely and said, "Thank you" to their hosts.

They had shared a week of bliss with Jim and Jane, who had pleaded with them to stay with them, as they made a good team. They had seriously considered the offer and had not made up their minds.

They were amused when Jim and Jane went to a keep fit group each Sunday afternoon at precisely 3pm. Why weren't they happy with their exercise bike? At least that kept the electric flowing!

They had learned that away from the house they had to have their wits about them. Not everybody attacked people at random, but enough did to make existence very precarious. They had not seen anyone armed with guns and bombs, but people had some very potent home-made weapons, using whatever they could find.

Fred and Julia had narrowly escaped a few beatings, in one case by being as brutal as the attackers, but when Jim heard, he had asked him not to do so again. It was safer in the long run to make as few enemies as possible and be as anonymous as possible.

Things had gone well until their third Tuesday with Jim and Jane. After two weeks of watching the thugs and learning how and when they would be most dangerous, they had managed to get out of the house for walks and thoroughly enjoyed being together. But on the fateful day their plans took a huge step backwards.

They had been walking on the usual route, along the shore and then along some roads that had not been too badly damaged. Then they heard a shout from about 80 metres away, "Hey, I know you. I bet you're not so bold now. Start to run!"

A gunshot rang out and they ran along a house path and between the houses. They continued to the back garden and over a wall. They kept on running over some rubble from demolished houses before they heard another shot. This one hit the rubble inches from them as they dived behind the remains of a tree, which still looked a lot healthier than anything else in the surrounding area! They made for some damaged houses and shops and started to go faster on a comparatively undamaged footpath. Their attacker had still been cursing them loudly and, as he made his way over the last of the rubble, he shot and gave Fred a flesh wound on his right thigh, but then the gunman slipped and fell into the cellar of a demolished house just before the clear area.

Fred and Jane had limped, walked and stumbled for about a further mile before they stopped and hid - and tried to decide what to do next. They could go back to Jim and Jane's, but didn't because if they were followed it would bring the wrong kind of attention to Jim and Jane. They were sorry that they could not say a proper 'Goodbye' to them, but they were concerned for Jim and Jane's safety. It was rare for either of them to consider anyone but themselves, but Jim and Jane had won them over.

. . . . .

Thirty kilometres away, in Preston, life had not got any easier. The group had imposed voluntary rations, but each one realised that they would have to cut their expectations even further. There were more and more people in the old Labour Club. So far they had not had to refuse anyone a meal or a place to sleep if they needed it. The Labour Club had become too small for them all so they had requisitioned two pubs in the immediate area. Before they took over the first, they announced at a meeting that they hoped to do so but asked if anyone knew who to contact for permission and what the likely cost would be. Greg, who had been part of the group recently, put his hand up and said, "Me."

The person leading the meeting said, "I'm glad somebody knows. Who is it?"

Greg said, "Me. I own it! You can use it for whatever you wish. No cost!

Greg had had a difficult life, but was a hard worker who had put all of his life into making a living from the pub, a friendly if occasionally rough pub that had housed the local Supporters Club for Preston North End Football Club. He had met Nigel Davies, who had occasionally dropped in to the Supporters Club. Nigel had tried to get him involved in the Chess Club, but despite Nigel telling him that it was much more than chess, he had remained to be convinced. He was about to commit suicide after the collapse of his business and the disasters when Nigel had met him and taken him to the

Labour Club. His life had become better in every way and he worked hard for his new friends.

In a very short space of time this second building was becoming too small and Greg asked his friend who owned the pub next door to volunteer his building. The answer was "OK, on condition that I can still live there."

The huge expansion meant that there were greater and greater demands on their supplies. They always managed to have enough food, but they never quite understood how or why, except that they trusted the Only One who could do something about it.

Nigel, JID's father, had taken on the task of organising the food provision. Various people offered food, usually bartering for some material favour or help in some way. The amazing thing that they saw was that even, in the most difficult of times, lots of people were prepared simply to give to the group and many became part of it.

JID was a person who had a level head and had a hard earned wisdom to deal with difficult situations. He was still involved with a forage group, but with the expansion of the work other groups had started to keep the hungry in basic essentials. JID and all the other people on the foraging groups would be away from Preston for between three and five days then stay put and rest for two or three days. He always looked forward to enjoying his rest days and having plenty of quality time with Ruth. Life was hard, but was very fulfilling.

. . . . .

Fred and Julia had walked from Blackpool, but didn't know what to do next. Any town would be likely to produce the same kind of violence they had met as they fled Blackpool. However, if they stayed in the countryside they would be more obvious targets for people being violent, either because that was how they lived or because they were among the many who had personal vendettas against him. They found what they could to eat in the mornings and evenings. They tried to stay under cover during the days and travelled at night - not having any idea where they were travelling to.

They got to the stage where they felt as weary as they had when they were paddling for their lives in the Irish Sea. They stayed put for a couple of days. They had already learned that haystacks were safe, warm and comfortable, so they made use of one. They ate whatever they could find- which was not very much. Each had thought of taking their meaningless lives, but they had not discussed it with each other, otherwise they might have arranged suicide together. They kept going because of care for each other and fear of death. Their instinct was that any life was better than death, although they were less convinced than ever.

After five days, longer than they had intended, Fred and Julia felt strong enough to take the next, perhaps the last part of their trek. They rose and ate their last apples. They were comfortably lounging on one side of the haystack when they heard someone some distance behind them calling, "Did you manage to find anything?

Somebody just the other side of the haystack, about five metres from them answered, "I've got some fruit and I have seen some cattle that look as if they have been abandoned. I think the others have done quite well too. We'll find out when they all get here.

Fred and Julia were terrified. This was not one or two people, but a gang. They would have climbed into in the haystack, but the noise would draw attention to them. They whispered to each other and decided to sit still and hope that they would not be noticed. They sat for perhaps half an hour, but it seemed like an eternity. The group were just one haystack away and they estimated that there must be about ten of them. They said that they would start to go back home when the last pair arrived. Eventually they arrived, but approached from the opposite direction from the others. They saw Fred and Julia from a distance and shouted, "Hi, how did you get on," thinking that they were part of their group.

They had been rumbled! There could be no hiding or fleeing now, and they were too weak to fight. They stood up and spoke to the group. The leader of that group was none other than Red Young. He and Kit had settled with the Preston group and his strength and energy had proved extremely valuable to the group. JID was popular and attracted people to his forage group, but, not surprisingly, more wanted to be in Red's group. Red had selected the younger, stronger ones who could forage further away from Preston.

Fred and Julia realised that they had better try to make peace with the group and hope that the group, unlike other groups he had encountered, would have mercy on them. He walked up to Red who was obviously the leader and, at 1.9 metres tall, stood out from the rest in more ways than one.

"Hello, you made our bedroom your meeting place," Fred said with a smile, hoping to disarm any hostile intentions they may have had. "Can we be of assistance to you?

Red smiled and replied, "I'm sure you can, but first perhaps you need our help!" He looked at the state of the couple and the wound on Fred's leg. They needed food, a wash and some method of getting rid of the effect of days in a haystack.

Red continued, "There is a stream on the other side of those woods. Have a bath and we'll have some hot food ready in half an hour. Have we got any clean clothes?" One of the group took a large pack off his back and produced clothes for them. It was a very warm day so they both did as they were told and went to the stream. They returned to find that there was enough beef stew for everyone including themselves. After giving some simple, but effective first aid the group turned for home.

The journey back to Preston was a difficult one. At some points they had to find another route or even double back to avoid attention from gangs. Julia walked the whole way, even though she found it hard to keep up with the group. Fred found the going harder and harder with his wounded leg and, to his embarrassment, had to travel a lot of the distance on a food cart being pushed and pulled by and Julia the uncomplaining group members.

They chatted with the group and found out a bit about each other's histories, but Fred and Julia only gave selected bits. When Red Young said who he was, Fred said, "I thought I had seen you somewhere! Sorry I couldn't say where! I have to admit that I am not a football follower."

"That's not important," said Red. "Football is not important to the most avid supporter now. There are more important issues at stake."

Two days later, on the Friday, they arrived in Preston. Fred's wound was turning septic, but would have been much worse if he hadn't met this group. On arrival in Preston they took him to the nurse in the Labour Club, who knew the best dressings and treatment for him. They both stayed in the medical department while they recovered from weakness and injuries.

JID's foraging party arrived back the day after Red. They discussed their recent journeys and their joys and failures. Red mentioned Fred and Julia, and hoped that they would appreciate God's work in their lives and ask for forgiveness and new lives. Red said that he was sure that Fred and Julia were keeping a lot of secrets about their past lives.

They prayed. JID prayed that, whatever Fred and Julia had done in the past, they would know the joy of forgiveness. He had learned that ANY sin, however evil, would be forgiven for people who said sorry to God and wanted to live new, forgiven lives. He thanked God that people could be reconciled to God and to others.

Later that evening Fred was in bed in the medical room with Julia by his side. They were talking with Red Young, who was on the side away from the door. JID was going to go into the room to meet Fred when he realised that he had already met him!

The people in the room had not noticed JID, who turned away and went to the kitchen. He found a broom and kicked the head off it, turned and strode purposefully towards the medical room. He entered the room, swung the broom handle and aimed at the head of 'Fred'. This was, in fact, Kenneth Kippam, the company torturer!

Despite having been hiking through the countryside dragging a cartload of food and human being the day before, Red was able to quickly dive over the bed without even touching it, as if wanting to head an opposing shot off the goal line. He pushed JID and his flying broom handle away from both Kenneth and Julia. Red and JID both recovered and got to their feet.

"What do you think you are doing?" grumbled JID. "You are sheltering a man who is worse than a murderer! This is the animal who imprisoned me for weeks and made my life hell! And there must be hundreds of others like me. He had a medical team, but even they were frightened of him. And he wasn't interested in my best interests. This man deserves what is coming to him - and if I can give him what he deserves it will save a lot of work for other people."

Red looked hard at JID with the intensity of his younger days when JID played badly. "Do you think that you are a Christian?"

JID said, "Yes, but extraordinary people need…"

Red interrupted, "Are you saved from wrong by God's goodness?

"Yes, but…"

"And were you praying for this couple, whatever they had done in the past?

"I didn't know what they had done, if I…

"Don't you know that Saint Paul was a thug for the organisations who tried to capture and silence Christians."

JID didn't know what to say. He knew that what Red was saying was right, yet his inside turned over at the thought of this creature ever being accepted by God or His people. What if they fed and clothed him, only for him to turn against the Church using the knowledge that he had gained about the group. This is the man who had no qualms about having him beaten up, left naked, dirty and probably drugged in solitary confinement, prevented him from having any contact with the outside world and trying to bend his mind.

Julia spoke. "We thought long and hard about what we were doing. We didn't decide one day to be evil."

JID realised that she was the one who was Kenneth's secretary, and had accepted his treatment as normal and unremarkable when he came out of his cell.

She continued, "It is the kind of work that creeps up on you. You are doing the paperwork about it. Then you see some of what happens. Then you get a promotion and find yourself talking to prisoners" (the first time anyone had admitted that they had kept prisoners) "and befriending them to get information. Eventually we were in charge of the whole operation."

JID was now a lot calmer. "You have no excuse!"

Before he could continue Kenneth said, "Yes. You're right. If you or anyone here decides to treat us as we treated you, I can have no complaint. My conduct was the worst imaginable. I am at your mercy and I will accept what you decide. We had actually left the organisation a few weeks after you had been held, and I changed my name for safety and to make a new start."

This admission took JID off his guard. He thought that Kenneth Kippam's way of acting had been so natural that he could not act any other way. Now the beast of Shopafrolic was eating humble pie! Was this just his way of playing for time? Then JID noticed that Kenneth had tears in his eyes! These were not the tears of physical pain - Kenneth's physical condition was rapidly improving. JID found it hard to equate the man in the bed with January's torturer - yet he had admitted that it had really been him.

JID started to weep and ran out of the room in embarrassment. In the last year he had had so many surprises, but this one was greatest of all by a kilometre. Was Kenneth actually changing? Was he really sorry about his actions? Was it right to pretend that nothing bad had happened? Was it right to get on with life without even a trial to determine what had happened? If he and others had been able to claim fair compensation even Kenneth Kippam would not be able to earn enough to pay in several lifetimes.

Later JID accepted Kippam as part of the group, despite his naturally bitter feelings. He was helped to that conclusion by Ruth, Red and other people who he would happily trust with his life. He found it almost impossible to forgive. It helped when he, Kenneth Kippam and Julia Crompton were alone in the Club and had a long talk. They had had greater and greater misgivings about their role and eventually withdrew from it. They told JID about Sao Lucia. (It's existence was not public knowledge.) They had been held in such respect by the companies that their names were on the list to evacuate to Sao Lucia should that ever become necessary! If things had gone well their pension, after 20 years work, would be equal to their normal salary. The only way they could escape the company was to claim that their independent company was to compliment the companies' work, and that the arrangement would be mutually beneficial to both them and the companies.

Shopafrolic let him go, but spent a lot of time stressing how much he would lose by the arrangement. That did not worry him, as he wanted to put the past well and truly behind him.

Although JID was still uncertain of their aims, he accepted Ruth's words, "If you were in his position and knew how powerful the companies were, would you have the guts to break away from them?"

He considered the question many times, but was still not sure of the answer.

# Chapter 10. October.
# A Bad Change and a Good One...

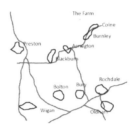

Life in Preston was becoming increasingly difficult. There was less food available out there, and no way to produce any food. It occurred to the foraging groups that it may be worthwhile trying to break in to some of the food factories and centres. Much of the food would, by now, be producing interesting toxic odours, but anything tinned or frozen may still be useful. It was known that a lot of factories had huge automatic generators powered by solar power and stocks of diesel fuel. There was a huge food plant near Wigan, and Red's group joined with another and set out to see what they could do.

When they arrived they found that they weren't the first to have had that idea. There was evidence that several people had attacked the eight metre high boundary fence earlier. They surveyed the scene and came to a plan of action. They found the Liverbean plant was a tough nut to crack. (Liverbeans were baked beans produced by Livershops). They started trying the obvious and usually most successful ploy, brute force! Ropes tied to fence posts or fence mesh would easily crumble under the combined pulling power of the two groups- they thought. But thought never moved a fence, especially this fence! Although the material of the fence looked like 1.0 millimetre steel, which should have buckled under such weight, or been cuttable with the right kind of shears, they couldn't even scratch or make a slight bend in the metal.

They tried forcing two pieces of mesh apart with some specialist devices one of the group had worked with in better days. It was a hand operated hydraulic jack, so the force could be gradually increased. It produced a huge force to force the fence bars apart. After hours of trying, with Red and the others adding their strength the lever on the machine gave way. The group gave a huge cheer, having beaten the fence, only to find that it wasn't the fence that gave way, but their hydraulic jack.

Another part of the group had been trying to burrow under the fence in an area where there was grass on the inside. They worked like slaves and used the skills of a civil engineering foreman on the group to keep the work carefully supported. Their hole was just 1.2 metres square, as every bit of subsoil had to be hauled out in buckets by rope and they wanted to minimise the volume they needed to move. They had taken as much timber as they could in case it was needed, and they used it to shore up the sides.

They had already descended to seven metres before they gave up from exhaustion and low morale. The fence still standing proud, and still there so far under the surface.

They had decided that if you couldn't get through or under, the only way was over.

They had been away for five days and decided that they would work Saturday, have Sunday off and restart on Monday. They sent home one of the group to tell the folk at base what was happening. She was 21 years old and couldn't carry great weights, but was in the group as she was good at seeing the way through problems and encouraging the others. With her wiry frame she had been a reasonable marathon runner, having completed the Megatrade Marathon in three and a half hours the previous year. She started to run towards Preston. All along the route she had been able to almost sense the presence of gangs and traps. When she offered to run to Preston, at first Red objected out of sheer old-fashioned chivalry, but she and the others prevailed on him and he reluctantly agreed.

The distance from Wigan to Preston was just right for a marathon runner, although she did about twelve more kilometres to keep on the safe side of possible trouble. She eventually arrived and told the bad news. JID and Ruth spent a lot of time with Kit and the others who quickly acquired the nickname 'Wigan Widows.'

Sadly, one of them was to become a real widow. Mushtaq had been born and spent his early life north of Peshawar in Pakistan. His family had not been troubled by extremists who were out fighting various Government forces most of the time. However, when Mushtaq was 6 years old his father inherited a lot of money from an uncle who had become wealthy in France, and they used the money to emigrate to England, as the countries were then known.

Until the recent disasters he had been a firm Muslim, with a great respect for Christianity. His wife, an NWE national of no real faith, became a Muslim for him out of genuine love for him before the marriage.

He often discussed religion with many kinds of people including some Christian friends. When the disasters started to happen he, like millions of people of varying faiths, somehow felt that he had better start taking the Christian faith seriously. He decided that Jesus was right in the things He said as the prophesies that He and others made in the Bible appeared to be happening. He read the Bible more carefully and listened more when his friends spoke. Eventually he decided to become Christian, at about the same time as his parents.

Mushtaq had never tried serious mountain climbing but he knew that he would be likely to have a better idea than any of the others because of his family's background in the Hindu Kush mountains. One of the group fashioned hooks from some (normal) steel bars they had salvaged the previous week, and they had attached these to ropes. Mushtaq put on solid boots and tied his boots to ropes with hooks on the other end. He held specially fashioned grappling hooks that had been made for the purpose. He was quickly able to ascend the fence. The rest of the group were cheering him on and some were pleading to be the next to climb.

Mushtaq got to within two metres of the top of the fence and simultaneously eight lasers shot him and turned his body instantly into a charred, shrunken mass, hanging upside down from the ropes. It was so unexpected and sudden that the others just looked amazed and didn't take in what had happened. After a few seconds and almost in time with each other they burst into action. Some collapsed on the ground in tears. Some decided that flight was right, in case the lasers were controlled by humans and not, as was probably the case, by mindless machines. Red went into leader mode and decided that in this situation the best thing would be to give himself a few more seconds to think. It was good that he did. Two group members started to climb towards the body to take it for a decent burial. Red came to the correct conclusion that, had they tried, they would have three bereavements to deal with. He managed to catch one before he reached the fence and yelled to the second, who came to his senses before he got too far.

The sad group got to Preston on the Wednesday and Red took on the responsibility of breaking the news to

Mushtaq's young widow, Millie. She was immediately distraught, but, over the next few minutes, she got enough composure to say, "When he was a Muslim he always said that he would be prepared to give his life for the true faith, although he said that he would not be prepared to kill. Now he has given his life trying to help others to live, just like Jesus. I hoped I would never lose him, but what better reason could there be?" She then thought about the situation again and collapsed in tears.

The group prayed with Millie while other people stored the meagre rations they had been able to gather on that trip.

During the next week it was decided that the food groups would go back to their normal salvage tasks and the idea of trying to break in to industrial premises would be abandoned for a while and then perhaps reconsidered. Their total weekly amount of food they found was very low. The reserves had almost been used up so, in the following days, the whole community voluntarily decided to carefully reduce their rations again. There was no need to set a formal limit as everyone realised the gravity of the situation, and they reduced their intake. They decided that the voluntary, but effective limit would only be relaxed for special occasions like the following weekend's event...

. . . . .

Saturday came - the date set for the wedding of Fred and Julia. Fred had decided to keep that name to show that his previous life was well and truly behind him. He had become popular with the other people in the Club and, by now, even JID was on good terms with him. There had been no interference or even any sight of Government, company or organised paramilitaries for several weeks, so they were able to plan the wedding without the kinds of precautions that had accompanied JID and Ruth's special day. The service would be one of the more recent ones produced just before the organised Churches became too compromised. Mark McCallow worked with them to get the details of the service and the whole thing was put together with the support of the whole community.

Two of the salvage groups did as well as could be expected, and Red's group did much better! They became the first people to discover a farmyard in a remote area of East Lancashire. They milked all the cows that produced any milk (to the great relief of the cows!). They slaughtered cows that didn't produce milk. The remaining cattle were looked after by a couple who stayed behind on the farm, for future use by the group. The discovery of the farm also produced various vegetables that the previous farmer and his family grew for their own consumption. There was no clue about the couple's whereabouts, but they had clearly abandoned the scene several weeks earlier. There were three old-fashioned carts, which had been regularly used in the early 20$^{th}$ century. Photos in the farmhouse showed that they were kept in reasonable order by the farmer who used to show them at local rural garden parties. There were several horses in a nearby field, and they were pushed into service to drag the carts, loaded with Red's very happy group and the various treasures that had been gathered during the operation. While some group members were controlling the carts, others used saws to cut parts of the cattle bodies into manageable pieces for cooking.

They approached Preston at record speed! As usual, they delayed to check for any paramilitary groups that may be using the M6 motorway, before proceeding along the underpass without incident.

A lot of the gangs in Preston had disappeared. Some gang members had died from malnutrition. Some had killed others. Some who were still in reasonable health had decided that they would have a better chance away from the town. Some gangs still existed and, as Red's group approached Preston, they met a reduced but still vicious gang.

This had been expected by the group, and they had drawn up a plan of action, which worked like clockwork! Red climbed down from his cart alone and approached the gang. Some recognised Red and were ready to talk. He left instructions that if he was caught by the gang they were to leave him there and escape. The other group members had objected - and both he and they were unsure what would happen if that scenario unfolded. They didn't need to find out.

Red sat down with the gang members and told them that they would all eat that day. He then went on to explain that they were part of a larger group in Preston.

He told them that if anyone wanted to join the group they would be welcomed, and would be able to take a share in a successful organisation that had been able to keep itself reasonably well fed ever since the disasters.

Three gang members said they were impressed and wanted to join. Red turned towards the wagon train and shouted, "Three". Two girls from the group dismounted the carts and walked half way between the carts and the gang. The three gang members (two men and a woman) were confident enough to go to talk with the group members. The group girls explained some facts about the group and how it worked, leaving the decision to them. All three decided to get on the carts and immediately offered to help to cut up the meat.

The other eight gang members became frightened that their gang would be smaller and started to complain to Red. Then they suddenly turned on him. He escaped their clutches and ran. He was considerably slower than he had been the last time he had been on a football pitch, but easily outpaced the gang members. Most of the missiles they flung only just missed him, but one gave him a bruise on the right arm. As Red approached the carts they started to move and Red scrambled aboard the last one.

At the same time, group members had kept Red's promise of food, thinking that it would put them off following the carts and leave them to peacefully organise the cooking and eating. They were half right. The group threw two large joints for each of the gang.

The gang stopped following the carts, but turned against each other in trying to get more than their share of the meat, which was the first they had seen for weeks. Some were so overcome by hunger that they started to eat the meat raw. The last the group saw of the gang was a huge fight and one girl looked as if she had been killed. While the group all felt distraught at the result of their encounter, they realised that there was nothing they could do to improve the situation and continued the last couple of kilometres to the Labour Club.

. . . . .

The next day, Thursday, was a day off for Red and his group. He was in the Labour Club on a comfy chair and his feet up on a stool. Fred, Ruth, Kit, most of Red's group and a few others were sat in a circle with him. Almost all of the group were in the three buildings. A fourth building was needed, and one, a former Megatrade store, seemed available. A group had been put together to assess the building and try to bring it up to the standard they needed. Almost the whole of the store's stock had disappeared since the disasters, leaving a large space that could be used for any purpose they chose.

Julia had gone out with a group visiting other sites in Preston for possible future use and didn't know about the Megatrade store.

Red and the others were talking about their faith and the state of the world. The last few months had provided many surprises and they that were convinced there would be a lot more to come. They were glad that they had found the extra food source, and were beginning to consider if it would be possible for some more group members to settle on the farm and perhaps make it a centre for salvage groups in that area. The possibilities seemed fascinating and all the group were fired up with excitement at those possibilities. Again, reality struck, this time in a way they had previously feared, but had since discounted.

Gunshots were heard at the outside door of the building. There was a lot of shouting. Someone yelled, "Keep still and put your hands up" to the people nearer the door. Some tried to escape the building but were shot by paramilitaries as they ran from the door. Three masked paramilitaries marched into the room where Red and the others were sitting, and they all looked up, alarmed, confused and frightened. One of the paramilitaries pointed to Fred and said, "That one!" in a strangely familiar voice. Red stepped in front of them to protect Fred and they shot him through the heart.

"Why, Julia???" shouted Fred to the commander of the unit, who was none other than his wife.

"Why do you think? The world is falling apart and you get involved with a load of religious weirdoes! At first I thought you had the sense to go along with them as far as you needed, and then turn them in. I played along with you and even had that feeble wedding ceremony for you, but I have been taking notes for your trial, if we decide to let you have one. Power is all that matters now and your 'New Way' plays human power down. The Kingdom, the power and the glory belong to the ones with the guts to take it, not to this miserable crowd, or their God," she said, pointing to the others who had a lot to say, but were in no position to say it.

Ruth was trying to comfort Kit, who had just seen her husband gunned down in cold blood, but when she started to talk to Kit a paramilitary shot five centimetres from her head and shouted "Shut up or I'll kill a few more."

Paramilitaries had flooded the building. Every person in the building, and the two satellite buildings had their mouths firmly taped and their hands Liverglued behind their backs. The paramilitaries formed them into a queue reminiscent of scenes of the treatment of Jews in the Second World War, and marched them off to Preston prison. They were forced to wash their hands in a solution which dissolved the glue, but also burned their hands. Their first task was to clear the prison of the bodies of prisoners. After the transporter disasters the warders had abandoned the prisoners and they had died of starvation. Every member of the Group, (male and female, strong and weak, sick and healthy) was forced into very hard labour. Julia, who had been a trusted and welcomed part of the group, spat at them and made sickening sarcastic comments.

The worst treatment was saved for Fred. A room had been specially prepared for him. It was not unlike the one where he had held JID, except that the floor was rough, sharp concrete. He shared the cell with cockroaches, ants and rats. The temperature was changed from a stingingly tropical 50° C to an Arctic -6° the whim of the torturer of the moment. His left hand was tied to the wall one and a half metres from the floor and his right hand below it, nought point three metres high.

The inquisitors tried for days to get Fred to deny his faith and his friends. He did neither.

Julia came in to the cell and had him untied. "It doesn't have to be like this," she said. "I love you as much as ever and I want to be able to go back to the way it should be". She put her arms round him and gave an apparently affectionate hug and kiss. He did not respond in any way.

"All you have to do is give us all the info you have on everyone here, and a list of anyone we have missed and we will be able to go to Sao Lucia and enjoy the high life!" She knew, but he didn't, that the Sao Lucia dream had ended up as a nightmare.

Fred didn't even complain about his treatment, and rued the days when he was in the torturer's seat. He had seen the ways successful prisoners had resisted him and he put all of their techniques into practice.

"My recognised name is Fred, formerly Kenneth Kippam. I am no longer connected to any military force and demand my freedom", was a ploy he had adopted from JID's time in his custody.

If it was his own safety he was concerned about he would probably have given up and told them what they wanted to know, but now he had two much greater motivations, of equal gravity. Firstly he would not betray his loyal friends. The Preston group had taught him that loyalty and concern for others (especially the ones who had looked after him so well and given him a job as an administrator) was much more valuable than all the wealth the world could give, even in the days when the world had had much more.

Secondly, and to his amazement, he appreciated God's love and the power He gave in these extreme circumstances.

. . . . .

JID's group returned the next day. All had seemed normal in Preston until they got near the pubs and saw bullet holes and smashed windows. They turned back and approached the Labour Club from another direction. It, too, had broken windows and there were some blood marks spattered around. JID told the group to wait at the back while he went to the front to get more idea of what had happened.

He carefully looked round the corner of the building at the front door and saw several bodies. He could see no sign of anyone alive and stepped towards the door, when someone called, "JID! Am I glad to see you!"

It was JID's father, who assured him that the attackers were now one day away. JID called for the rest of the group to join them.

"A gang of guerrilla - morons attacked yesterday. They shot people near the door and I was one of them. I can't remember anything since. I came round, but can't walk. I've got bullets in both legs. I do not know where everyone else is."

JID and the group helped Nigel into the building and put him into the bed in the treatment area. Mike, the group's first aid man did what he could.

Reality then set in for JID. If the buildings had been attacked, what had happened to Ruth and the rest? He panicked and ran round the building. Nobody was alive there, but Red and several others were dead. Ruth was nowhere to be seen.

They did a careful search of all the buildings with no result. What they did find was a few notes about the new building. They knew that Julia did not know about the possibility of using the Megatrade building, as the two property groups had a friendly rivalry and didn't discuss what they had in mind with each other until their plans were almost fulfilled, so JID and his group members took all they could use from the Labour Club and the two pubs and went to the supermarket.

After being crowded out in three buildings, there were now just fourteen people in a building big enough to hold a thousand. They saw the advantage of having plenty of places to hide if paramilitaries or anyone else turned nasty against them. They sent a smaller group than usual to the country farm to bring provisions for the few who were left. The rest stayed in Preston to make the supermarket as comfortable as possible. They were considering going to the farm, but they didn't want to leave the area in case any of the ones who had disappeared turned up.

It was a hard time for them all. JID, his father and three others had lost their wives or husbands and didn't know if they were dead or alive. They had plenty of food but most of it was 45 kilometres away across what now seemed forbidding countryside. They tried to think clearly but had so many conflicting thoughts, motivations and emotions.

. . . . .

In Preston prison, less than a kilometre from the supermarket, the torture continued. Some apparently relented and offered to give information. They then gave lots of wrong information to confuse the inquisitors. That only led to more horrendous treatment after their subterfuge was investigated.

The torturers had never met a group quite like this one. With any group of over 200 people there were always some who would wilt under the strain of persecution.

With the Preston Christians that didn't happen, even the ones who had only just joined. They told their persecutors that God loved them! They even told the persecutors that they also loved them despite their despicable lifestyle. They discussed the local situation, what they knew of the world situation and anything else they wanted to talk about. But when it came to betrayal, they would have no part in that.

One woman torturer, Eva Bingham, broke down in tears while she was doing her job! She said sorry to the man she was dealing with, immediately stopped her work and asked if he and God could possibly forgive her. The man was briefly stunned into silence, and he thought she was using a ploy to make him drop his guard and say things he would regret. Then he looked into her eyes and realised that her conscience had been scarred and she wanted to change. She untied his ropes, which had held his limbs in very cramped positions for the last four hours. She quietly asked if he would prefer to sit in her chair (a very comfortable armchair) or lie down on a bed near the corner. He decided to lie down as he had no strength to sit up. It was only half an hour, two cups of tea and several biscuits later that he managed to sit up straight.

As soon as he was on the bed the conversation took a strange turn. She explained that the sounds from the cell must sound like genuine torture, or they both would be in serious trouble. He said he would cooperate. They would talk quietly about the more important matters. He thought her motives were good and he was happy to talk of his faith, but he was not yet convinced enough to place his friends in danger by giving her any info about them. The discussion went like this:

"ARE YOU STILL TRYING TO DEFY ME? ANSWER ME." (Sound of a whip-crack, and a loud groan.)

"Life does not make sense for me any more. I'LL TRY YOUR FAVOURITE TORTURE."

"NO, DON'T DO *THAT* AGAIN." (A bitter scream followed.) "I am not surprised! We were created to follow Christ and we have something seriously wrong without Him. NO, DON'T. HOW CAN A WOMAN HAVE SUCH BITTERNESS? IT'S INHUMAN."

She cracked the whip several times and he screamed each time. They both became amused by their charade, and had to try very hard not to burst into hilarious laughter. The conversation continued for the remaining 30 minutes of the scheduled session and, with the torture sound effects removed, went something like this:

"My parents were regular Church-goers and wanted me to be the same. I went each week until I was 16 and got bored, although I knew I was letting them down. I also knew that God, if there was one, wouldn't be very happy. I was gambling with my life and put my money on atheism. I became a career woman and had lots of affairs with no one matching my extreme selfish standards. Still, the last thing I wanted was to be tied down in work, romance or anything else. It's only in the last couple of years that I have begun to be lonely. I'm 36 and wanted time to find the right man. When I saw an advert for this job a year ago I was intrigued. I've got a copy of it here. (She showed it to the man.)

# Northwesteurope Government / Company Partnership

Interesting Work for the
Smooth Running of Society
£9,500 per hour plus bonuses.
Hours to suit yourself.

Are you able to work
with minimum supervision?
Are you a problem solver?
Do you like working with people,
while not necessarily liking them?
Do you understand peoples' motivation?
Are you prepared to take on secret projects?
Are you unfazed
by surprising or difficult situations?
Will you sign and be bound by
the Official Secrets Act?

If the answer to all these questions is 'Yes',
you may be our person for the job.
If so, phone 0151 777 5304
in the next 24 hours!

"I mentioned the advert to other people in the office. They looked in their version of the news on paper and screen, and the space where this advert appeared was taken up by a Livershop dog-food promotion. Two people in the office dialled the number only to be told that the number did not exist. Later I 'phoned it from the same 'phone and the man at the other end said, 'Hello, Miss Bingham. I've been expecting a call from you!' and he said the job was mine if I wanted it!

"From that moment I was hooked! In seven hours of work I could get one month's pay at my previous rates, and the work, though undefined, promised to be fascinating. I gave in my notice for the middle-management job I had held down for a couple of years and followed the instructions that were relayed to me. It all seemed very 'cloak and dagger!' I would get text messages telling me to go to different places at different times, each one giving me slightly more information about the work without going fully into the dirty details. I was sucked into the organisation and then into this work.

"After the disasters the organisation seemed to collapse, but began to reform again under new management. Middle ranking people who had not been invited to Sao Lucia realised that there was a power vacuum and took their chance. I got a letter slipped under my door telling me to turn up at Preston prison the next day at 9.30am. 'Your life depends on it!' it said. That is their way of making an offer you can't refuse! They caught up with Julia and Fred, each not knowing that the other had been approached. Fred stood firm and Julia didn't.

"I am sick of the work and I want 'out'. Having seen your people under suffering I can see that you must have the answer - or at least think that you do so much that you will go through anything for it."

The intermittent litany of whip-cracks, insults and groans continued in the background to her confessions. Then he started to talk:

"There is nothing more important than this. If you want real excitement the first thing you do is accept that you are a sinner."

Those brief sentences were the prompt that made her collapse in a loud display of uncontrollable weeping. It sounded just right for convincing everyone else that torture was happening, even if the weeping may have sounded too feminine to be convincing, but neither was too worried about that at the time.

He continued to explain, in simple terms, what the Christian faith was about and prayed with her.

When the session was due to finish she, an accomplished artist, drew some very realistic 'bruises' on him using water and dirt from the floor of the cell.

She thanked him and went away in tears. She didn't chain him to the cell and assured him that she would be tomorrow's 'torturer'. When she got to the top of the steps he heard a man ask why she was weeping. She said that she had slipped over and hurt her leg and that it was nothing to worry about!

The next day she turned up with half of her own food ration for her prisoner, equivalent to more than three days of his normal rations.

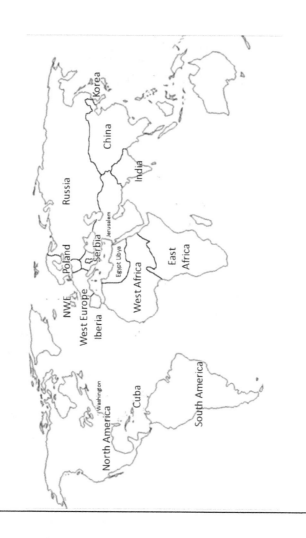

# Chapter 11. November.
# A Birthday and a Disaster...

"My birthday is fast approaching!" roared Gonzales as he addressed his men in the dining room of the Excelsior. The men cheered even louder than their leader and the rhythmical handclap followed. Gonzales and his tactical group had been discussing the operation between themselves and with each other, gradually refining their plans. One thing that Gonzales had failed to do was to have any meaningful discussions with either side in the Middle East so, as he talked to his men, he didn't even know which side he would fight for, but he wasn't concerned about trivial details. The few remaining Nation States were all so busy negotiating with each other and the still mighty armies of some collapsed States, that they had no patience with a few hundred terrorists with guerrilla skills, but with no real battle experience. They had forgotten that the guerrillas had taken and held parts of several major capitals including Washington in the last few years.

Gonzales flicked a switch and maps of the Middle East flashed onto the walls. Jerusalem was at the centre and the main concentration of armies was about 80 kilometres to the North. The old intercity Roads 66 and 65 meet near the town of Megido and the various forces held a standoff around that junction. Circles and arrows showed the positions of various armed forces already there. Israel forces were shown in light blue. They currently held the land between Jerusalem and the River Jordan.

Russia, with Cuba and various ex-Soviet states had advanced southwards between the Caspian Sea and Black Sea and were shown in red.

A huge force from China (yellow) had marched, some of them for over 7,000 kilometres, and was now stationed to the east. More than half had died of disease, exhaustion and hunger, but there were still many millions left.

Dark blue showed a few NWE and lot of American forces in Cyprus, in various parts of Israel and on some ships in the Mediterranean. They also had a smaller base to the west of the road junction.

Arab and African forces had joined and advanced from the south. Some remained to the south of Israel and some were marching northwards through Jordan.

Since the disasters, and the collapse of normal society throughout the world, the largest type of group that held together was the armed forces. They had some sort of discipline even if their discipline couldn't match the discipline of earlier years because of the general malaise of societies. They also had some supplies which had been stored for just such an emergency. For many years, even in many places where there was huge poverty, the rulers, for their own safety, always made sure that their forces were well-paid compared to everyone else and well-supplied with food and weapons. (That was the only way for rulers to hold on to military rule). Some had kept their conventional aircraft from previous days.

Supplies were running low for all the forces, but the officers had deliberately given the impression that all would be well if they were successful in this mighty war. 'To the victor the spoils,' was the general thinking and proclamation to their soldiers. They successfully used rhetoric and techniques tried for thousands of years, but which had never quite fulfilled the warrior's dreams.

"Why are we a bigger player in all of this?" Gonzales asked, rhetorically to his men. "It is because we have a weapon that is so simple yet so deadly. When we aim this beam towards a gun or weapon it will affect the electronic systems in the weapons and they will fire!" he said, stressing the last three words. "We can use it to fire remote weapons of our own so that our men will be safe when the enemy attacks the weapons. Or we can use it to make enemy weapons fire, so that they kill their own forces or selected other targets they happen to be pointing at. We will be able to fire guns, missiles and bombs (usually other peoples') by the flick of a switch!"

He pointed his device, which looked similar to a mobile 'phone, at a wall and pressed the red button. Within seconds the sound from a huge bomb on the other side of the bay shook the room, and the soldiers first went into defensive mode, simultaneously diving to the floor and drawing pistols. They then realised that this was Gonzales' demonstration of the new weapon. They cheered their leader for showing, yet again, that he was one step ahead of whatever opposition was out there.

"I had not had to test this weapon to see if it worked, my scientists have done that", enthused Gonzales. "All I had to do was pick one of the Iberian bombs that were already on the island at random. It was put in place, without any modification, and I used this device. It would work against any weapon with any kind of electronic control. Only soldiers without electronic devices, mainly African and some of the Chinese forces, will be free from this kind of attack! And they do not have the ability or tactics to beat you, my friends, in a gunfight.

"My new weapon, the 'Chaos Ray', must only be used with my permission. Before I give permission I will advise you and any friendly forces of its use so that, if necessary, any weapons can be pointed in an appropriate direction. And just to remind you of its power...'

Gonzales pointed the Chaos Ray at a machine gun lying on the ground. It started to fire and spun round firing in all directions. In a split second one of his men dived from his seat and grabbed the gun, pointing it to the ground.

"A promotion for that man!" shouted Gonzales. "He did not know that the gun was one of the exercise variety, but he knew what to do to be on the safe side!"

"One more thing," said Gonzales, more quietly, "the Chaos Ray has a range control. You can set it for any distance between 20 metres and ten kilometres. It also has an angle control. You can send a single very direct beam or you can send the spread up to 30° from the centre. If you are unsure of your geometry, now is the time to learn.

That night every man in the force checked up his understanding of angles and distances.

. . . . .

When gravity-reversal failed, the NWE aircraft carrier (HMS Mechanica) was in mid Atlantic doing manoeuvres with other European and North American navies. 'Aircraft carriers' did not carry aircraft since the coming of gravity-reversal transportation. They carried men, machines and even a fleet of medium- sized sea vessels within their modified hulls. The plan was that much of the navy was at ease in the one mighty vessel, but at the slightest hint of danger the smaller vessels could be launched and would become part of a large flotilla. One of the two American aircraft carriers also took part in this exercise.

They were sailing towards each other from opposite sides of the Atlantic and were due to meet with craft from Iberia, Western Europe, Japan and elsewhere. The whole scenario was to have been a grand show for the 3Dvids. There were cameras everywhere on all of the ships so that the viewers would be able to be a virtual part of the action. The thinking of the companies and Governments was that the more you kept the masses tied to their 3Dvids the less likely they were to ask any really telling questions that the Governments were unable to answer.

Gravity-reversal failed and the transporters fell from the sky, but they didn't always fall in a straight line. Their computation systems, searching for the right electronic messages, took them either towards or away from any electronic systems depending on their polarity compared to the navigation systems on the transporters. Many transporters were attracted towards electric power lines, but tended to be sent away from generating plants. 3Dvid relay stations were almost all demolished.

One major attraction for the crazy, uncontrolled machines was sea transport - and the bigger the better!

Some small ships, the size of a trawler or smaller survived. Bigger ships were a much bigger attraction. Something the size of an aircraft carrier had no chance!

Any single transporter landing on an aircraft carrier would do serious damage, but would probably not sink it. On the fateful day each aircraft carrier in the entire fleet was bombarded by between 15 and 30 Transporters, some twice the size of a Boeing 848.

All that was left of the fleet was a few smaller rescue dinghies and patrol boats. They were unable to contact their base commanders so they followed their default orders for such an event and sailed for the Eastern Mediterranean, as that was where trouble on a large scale was the most likely to arise. Some ran short of fuel on the way and made for the nearest port. A few reached the Eastern Mediterranean.

The general plan of armed forces to go to the Middle East was worldwide. Even the vast armies of the Korean Peninsula stopped eyeing each other for a while and decided that they should join forces and make the huge trek westwards. Only a few made the whole journey as most had killed each other off when their national pride took over again and, perhaps predictably, warfare between the armies erupted.

. . . . .

Gonzales told his men of the travel plans. They would travel on one massive 848 plane. On the flight most of the men, like most of the others near Megido, had the numbers 6665 tattooed on them. It was a tradition for military personnel to have tattoos of the names of places they visited. The scenario was at the junction of routes 66 & 65.

Waiters from the island would care for their needs when they travelled, and the civil pilot would land the plane in Ovda airport in the south of Israel after they had bailed out. Gonzales had assured the pilot that this airport was operating as a passenger airport because of the efficiency of the Israeli Government reacting quickly when the problems occurred. Gonzales knew that it was very unlikely that the airport was, in fact, operational. To make sure that the pilot didn't aim the aircraft at his troops when he realised, Gonzales fixed bombs on the aircraft set to explode five minutes after his men had bailed out.

Bailing out of a huge passenger aircraft was not easy! The slowest that the pilot could safely fly that huge aircraft without stalling was over 450 kilometres per hour. He was flying at an altitude of about 300 metres at the time. It would normally be impossible to open the aircraft doors in flight, but a special device was designed to allow the pressure inside the aircraft to gradually decrease to the surrounding pressure of the air. The suits that the men wore, again designed specially, included breathing apparatus and they supported the paratroopers' bodies against the worst of the shock when they suddenly hit the 450 kph wind.

The plans went well and all but three of the men survived the descent. Another had a badly sprained ankle, so Gonzales shot him. They landed over an area of 15 square kilometres and started to walk towards a prearranged meeting point.

The men already knew the basic drill. All would approach the meeting point with extreme caution. The first there would place a green and blue flag to ease navigation for the rest. They would then start to reccy the area for other forces, or evidence that they had been there. There was plenty of evidence of that! The whole area was covered with food cans, weapons, excreta and occasional bodies. This scene was an encouragement to Gonzales! As he looked at the mess around him he was sure that at least one of the armies involved was much less prepared for the battle than were he and his men.

He then started much more detailed spying out of the area. The main group were barracked covering an area of five hectares. Guards took their turn round-the-clock to check on others in the area. The main soldiers with an immediate job to do were his Specialistos. They had an SAS-type of role. They went out in small groups under cover, trying to find out as much as they could about their potential friends and enemies. When they reported back the next step would be debated.

. . . . .

Noir, Simons and another man were one of the spying trios. Simons was chosen because he was a particularly good linguist. As they looked around and began to take in the situation from a hillside they were amazed at the scene. The whole area looked like a series of inter-school, seven-a-side football competitions. It was clear that nobody was expecting a major battle, or even a playground skirmish! Most of the troops looked weak and hungry. Some looked weak, hungry and determined to enjoy their football as they had nothing else to do. It seemed that these groups on this side of the road junction had formed allegiances.

The third man in the trio was sent back to Gonzales with a progress report. Noir and Simons saw no potential problems in venturing into the camp. They saw signs that some of the troops there were British, and decided to play along. They started to talk to some soldiers about the football. One told them, "Our first team did well against the Westeuropeans, beat them 5-1, but were beaten by the United Africa third team. They had men from all over West Africa. We play a Saudi team tomorrow and a couple from East Asia the next week. If we get to the final playoffs we will play against the top teams from the other three sectors and eventually we will find a winner. I don't reckon we have much chance!

"When will the final be?" asked Simons.

"Are you out of touch with everything? It's been the only thing of any interest since we got here!"

Simons thought quickly and said, "We've only just arrived here. We were sent south by the CO to look for good food sources, but we couldn't find much."

"The final's planned for February or March. The whole thing depends on how quick each quarter manages to hold its local league matches.

"I think the Russians will do well," ventured Simons, trying to get a greater idea of the whole scene.

"They are in the north sector. There are some European teams who are quite good in the north, teams from Serbia and Poland, you know, places round there.

Noir and Simons could hardly believe what they were witnessing. It seemed that the armies to the west of the road junction regarded football at the standard seen on any park on Saturday morning as the most important thing on earth. That evening they crept up to the CO's tent to see if they could glean any information about what mattered most - the military plans. There were already three men in the tent when the CO walked in. They all stood at attention until the CO said, "At ease, please sit down. We have important matters to discuss!"

Noir and Simons could hardly believe their luck, and gave a thumbs-up to each other. They switched on recorders so that Gonzales would be able to hear every word. The CO had a distinctive voice, but they couldn't tell the others apart.

"First, food. Did we manage to direct any more to where it will be needed most in the next few days?" asked the CO.

"No", said another, "but I think that the ones not involved in the action could be persuaded to slightly reduce their rations for this sally. We will need the task force plus others to be brought in if required. We will be expecting a lot if we think that we will be sure to get through this mission without casualties.

"Medicine should be OK?" asked the CO.

A voice in the tent said, "The best medical men will be on hand if needed. The Meds have already decided which teams to have available. They will have two teams of two personnel each. It's quite possible that they will not be needed, but you can never be sure, so they will be on standby in case."

"And what is the overall game plan for this?" asked the CO.

"Grant will be in goals again. He had a trial for Aston Villa when he was younger, but they had two international goalkeepers at the time and he had no chance. He played in League 2 for Southport before he decided to join the forces…"

Recorders were switched off and when the football discussion faded to be replaced by snoring, the spies withdrew and decided to try the sector to the west of the road junction the next day. The story was the same.

Nobody had any interest beyond football and the next meal. The various commanding officers had no plans for any action.

When they returned to base the other spying team had done a similar extensive survey of the other two sectors and came back with the same story.

. . . . .

When he got the news Gonzales was amazed and, for once, was speechless and deep in thought for several minutes. Eventually he spoke.

"Why do they come to a battlefield if there will be no battle?" said the seething Gonzales in a quiet menacing tone. "All they think of is the World Cup? The FOOTBALL World Cup! With serving soldiers who should be ready to do, die and kill!"

"FOOTBALL!" he roared! "We will give them a game to remember! And the score will not be counted in goals."

A plan quickly began to develop in Gonzales' mind. But first he wanted to give all his men a chance to add their thinking to the overall plan. He called a meeting for that evening.

. . . . .

Gonzales sat at the end of the huge marquee, which acted as home, mess and meeting room for his men, while some who had already had a briefing on the planned meeting formed a cordon and did guard duty.

The men had already been told of the situation near Megido eight kilometres to their east by the spy teams, but Gonzales told them about it anyway. He then asked, "If that is the situation what will we do about it?"

The suggestions ranged from leaving well alone until fighting broke out to an all-out Gung-ho attack with Chaos- Rays ablazing at the first opportunity! Most of the ideas were better thought out and more practical.

Gonzales said that he would consider the possibilities and they would re-convene at the same time the next day. They did, and all the men approved. The meeting was held on 4th November and their action planned for the following day. "Appropriate because in NWE they have fireworks that day!" said Gonzales. "We will start with the English!

The plan was that, for a few days, they would have fun with the Chaos Ray before they would start the real action. This particular plan would not have worked with some armies. In places like Afghanistan where random shooting of rifles for no apparent reason was considered the norm, an odd shot would be ignored. However, to quote Gonzales, "The British do not like that sort of thing."

Grant, the NWE goalkeeper was doing his last guard duty before laying down his arms to concentrate on training for the next match. He was just outside the camp and looking bored out of his mind. A couple of other men, both unarmed, came to him and started to talk.

Gonzales and the whole group were watching from a hillside about two kilometres away. Gonzales carried the only Chaos Ray machine they would use that day, set 0° spread. He put it on a stand and pointed it in approximately the right direction. He adjusted the sights until it seemed right, then went to a higher magnification. After the third tweaking of sights he pressed the switch that would follow Grant's rifle, and waited for the right moment.

Grant was not caring where his rifle was pointing, and the firing of the rifle was the last thing on his mind. He was laughing and joking with his friends, following the guidelines and keeping the rifle over his shoulder, pointing upwards to empty space. Some of Gonzales' men were trying to get him to shoot the ray somewhere else rather than sit around waiting, watching nothing through their high-magnification binoculars.

"Wait, our time will come! Be patient," said Gonzales. Sure enough, after thirty minutes one of the other men offered Grant a cigarette. Grant's mind went off his rifle while he lit up, and he let the rifle swing from the strap on his shoulder. Gonzales pounced by the press of a switch, and a bullet ripped through the CO's tent. Nobody in the NWE camp knew what had happened except the men who were with Grant. Even Grant did not realise that it was his weapon that had fired the shot. All the men in the NWE camp hit the deck, and two or three who were actually armed took out their weapons ready for action.

The CO had, through no skill of his own, avoided the bullet by 20 centimetres. He forgot about common sense and immediately ran out shouting that the man who had aimed at him was on a charge. He then saw that the rest of the camp were belly - down expecting further shots, and decided with the rest of the men that discretion was the better part of valour!

"It's OK! The guard's rifle went off on its own!" shouted one of Grant's friends.

"Nonsense!" shouted the CO, "do you take me for an idiot?"

At that, the entire camp tried very hard not to laugh, and a few failed.

"It's true, sir," said one of the other friends.

"You two are on a charge as well," said the CO, trying to regain the situation. He called for the Military Police, those specially trained thugs who combine strength and intellect with a murderous streak. They severely beat up Grant and the other two who were also stars of their football team, and led them away to the previously unused punishment tent where the summary punishment continued.

One of the other soldiers ran to the CO and said that they were mistreating three of the football team, so the CO ran to the punishment tent and told the MPs to stop. One, a former employee of Shopafrolic, who just a few months before had broken JID's ribs, glared at the CO and said, "and who's going to make me?"

"I'm your commanding officer!" he yelled.

"I don't care if you are Idi Amin. If I do not get £100,000 and double rations I'll break all of Grant's fingers this minute."

"Don't be ridiculous. I can't treat you differently to the rest!"

Grant squealed as his fingers were stretched even further back.

"Alright," shouted the CO, not out of care towards Grant, but his desire to win the next match.

The thug released Grant's fingers and the CO quickly drew his pistol and shot him and another of the MPs dead, but the third MP shot and killed both Grant and the CO. He pointed the gun at the other prisoners and told them to make themselves scarce. He only needed to suggest it once.

. . . . .

On the hillside Gonzales and his men chuckled. As they watched they saw that one stray bullet had caused mayhem in the British ranks. They were even more elated when they saw bodies being carried out- including the CO. Then Noir recognised Grant, and shouted that the team's star goalkeeper had also been killed.

"Round one to Gonzales!" shouted Gonzales! "What will tomorrow bring?"

. . . . .

The tank that became the target was the third of seven chosen by Gonzales. He guessed that if he picked seven tanks at least one of them would be likely to be loaded for action. The first two he tried were not loaded.

An old, but updated tank belonging to the Egypto-Libyan army was on one side of the hill, with its gun pointing lazily downwards. On the other side of the valley were the vast ranks of the Chinese army. There were always some soldiers of various nationalities, but there were mainly Chinese, bathing in the reservoir at the bottom.

He picked a time when there were about fifty Chinese enjoying their baths, along with a hundred or so others.

Gonzales handed the weapon to Noir and he went through the aiming procedure, focussing on the tank at a range of about 600 metres. The tank's weapon was not loaded with live ammunition, but with training rounds. When fired they sounded very real, but ejected no weapon.

One of the techniques that the Chinese always used was to defeat the enemy by sheer weight of numbers. No matter what arms they faced, if they had enough soldiers (and they always did) sooner or later their men would overwhelm their opponents.

When the tank fired, the Chinese men in the reservoir immediately grabbed their pistols and knives, and walked towards the North Africans, who were just as stunned as everyone else at their tank misbehaving. It took them precious seconds before they realised that the Chinese in the reservoir had been joined by countless thousands of their compatriots and were now running at an incredible speed towards their ranks.

The North Africans gathered their wits as soon as they could and manned the tank. They shut the hatch so that they would not have unwelcome visitors and armed it with real shells.

Meanwhile the Chinese had reached the North - African tents. They slaughtered any man they found, but soon the North - Africans had gathered their wits and started to use their weapons, which were left over from their last autocratic dictators - now slightly outdated, but still very effective. They kept on defending and the Chinese kept on attacking.

The loss of life on the Chinese side was about three times the entire strength of the North African army, yet they won the battle. The only survivors of the North African army were the ones who were able to get clear of the battlefield and mingle with other armies.

Gonzales and his men marched back to their tents, doing their trademark rhythmic clap all the way, and laughing and joking like children at the fairground.

"Round two?" asked Noir.

"Round two is a success! Now for round three." declared Gonzales.

. . . . .

Spies told Gonzales that the mood in all the camps had changed. The Indians were in the northern sector six kilometres from the road junction. They, like several other armies held 'suitcase bombs'. These were tactical nuclear weapons that were easily transportable. The Indians had been having their own cold war with China for many years. Although there had been no real military confrontation between the nations they didn't trust each other. When they realised that the Chinese had confronted and defeated a nation at random, for no apparent reason, they thought that the Chinese may choose to pick on them next.

The response was that the Indians sent 20 teams of three men each towards the Chinese army. Each team carried a 'suitcase bomb'. The US forces got wind of the Chinese attack and decided that they would send all their forces to join those to the west of the road junction. They did not know what to expect, so they took their supplies of nuclear weapons just in case the situation turned ugly.

. . . . .

As the tension was now very high, Gonzales decided, with the full approval of his men, that they would limit their attacks and let the other armies sweat in the uncertainty of the situation. Football stopped as the nations eyed each other suspiciously. It was the carefree West Africans who decided it was time to put things right. They arranged for their first team to play a team from Western-Europe in a show match. The two teams, which were evenly matched, would meet at a pitch specially set out at the road junction on 17$^{th}$ November. This would symbolically say to every side that peaceful coexistence was possible. They sent messages to all the other armies proclaiming that peace was possible and this match would prove it.

Gonzales had other ideas. This was to be a bigger and better scenario than anything seen before.

The 17$^{th}$ November arrived and, for the first time for over a week, the whole area had an air of calm. Lots of soldiers from many armies watched from the hills around, and the supporters of the teams watched from hastily built scaffolding behind each goal. Because of the message of peace that this game was to bring, the bigwigs of the armies involved became part of the build-up to the match.

Before the kickoff the badges of the armies were exchanged, not by players, but by their commanders. The PA system had a speech by them and by the referee from China, all translated into the native tongues of each army by one of their intelligence men.

It had been decided by others that the Israeli commander and the Iranian one should shake hands before the kickoff to further reinforce the message, but that proved to be one step too far, so they each gave a PA message from the opposite sides of the pitch.

The match started and went well. Both sides played robust games, but with great sportsmanship. The Africans were 1 - 0 ahead at half time after a wickedly swerving free kick from just outside the area sent the WE goalkeeper the wrong way.

The second half started, and Gonzales had planned to do his tricks five minutes into the second half. Some of his men were getting excited about the match and were betting each other about the next goal, the scorer, the next corner kick and various other events of the game. Some were actually enjoying the game for the football. They pleaded with Gonzales to let them watch until near the end of normal time. Gonzales, wanting to keep his men on- side, agreed, but said that when he said 'fire', they would fire without asking any further questions.

Gonzales' men were now on-side, but the African striker wasn't when he thought he had doubled the lead 20 minutes into the second half.

At 75 minutes, Gonzales ordered his men to aim their Chaos Rays and wait for his orders. The Chaos Rays held by ten of his men were set to fire any weapon within a circle of 200 metres from the centre spot. The men had learned to wait for the final moment patiently, to fit Gonzales' timing. Meanwhile, some of the men continued to watch the match avidly, but this time not as avidly as Gonzales.

He took in every move, but more than that, every emotion evoked by the play.

The WE team held possession much more than the Africans for most of the second half but only notched up a few half - chances. Then, in the $82^{nd}$ minute, a Westeuropean centre from the right touchline fell right towards their striker. The referee did not see the incident that followed as there was a man in his way, but the French supporters behind that goal saw it only too clearly. An African defender punched the striker in the ribs and he fell down in pain. The ball drifted past for a goal - kick.

The crowd behind that goal were furious and started shouting a lot of French at the referee.

Gonzales' moment had arrived! "FIRE" he yelled. Less than 10% of the football fans had taken their arms to the match, but that was enough. Guns fired all around the stadium. Many shot the people immediately round the guns, and a few hit people further afield. In the following confusion the Africans assumed that it was the French who were retaliating for not getting a penalty. Every African gun was then aimed at the French who retaliated in kind. The referee ran towards the PA system to appeal for calm, but fell when shot before he reached the touchline.

"Time for home and an early night!" said Gonzales, the commander of the one force never suspected of causing the mayhem! His men marched, grinning broadly - and hearing shots and explosions for several hours.

. . . . .

In the days that followed the tension was higher than ever. If a man sneezed anywhere within ten kilometres of the road junction, rifles would be pointed at him by his own men and anyone else within hearing distance.

Gonzales decided it was time for more fun, and set the date for 25$^{th}$. The suitcase bombs that various armies had on standby were very cunningly disguised. Some were kept in fridges or filing cabinets. Some were buried just below ground level, to be uncovered and used at a few moment's notice. Others were in tanks and other vehicles. Most had some sort of missile nearby to direct the weapon and they too were camouflaged.

Gonzales had decided to explode either an Israeli or an Iranian bomb, but hadn't decided which. After a long discussion with other leaders of his private army he decided that the best answer was 'both!' His explosive experts assured him that they would be safe at that range, but it would be best to march in the opposite direction to the blasts as soon as they happened to avoid getting involved with any crazed armies fleeing the scene. They had a ten kilometre start.

His men were to be at the maximum range of the Chaos - Rays, with a very precise pinpoint aim at the weapons. He and his men marched ten kilometres south of the Israeli lines, and Noir took his men ten kilometres north of the Iranians. They took up their positions and each waited over five hours until it was time to fire. In that time they set the precision aiming devices and checked the sights every hour. Everything was perfect.

At 7.06am the buttons were pressed. Gonzales and his men were waiting to hear two huge explosions, one slightly after the other about thirty seconds after the blast, but they heard nothing. The blasts from the Israeli and Egypto-Libyan bombs set off every single weapon in a huge area by physical forces that were unknown to scientists and had, of course, never been tested in any laboratory. Never before had more than one nuclear device been detonated at the same time. Now hundreds were detonated together, and the force of the total explosion was far greater than the sum of its parts.

An area of about 600 square kilometres was immediately flattened, and both of Gonzales' groups were caught in it. Centred on the road junction there was a huge crater over 100 metres deep and three kilometres in diameter. The mountains in the immediate area were unrecognisable, having had the tops shaved off.

. . . . .

Later JID was sitting in the supermarket considering what to do next. His father Nigel, JID's forage group and a few others who escaped the attack on the building were there - 17 people altogether. They had just about managed to stay alive by using whatever they could salvage from outside and a few scraps from the supermarket. They had been overjoyed at their latest discovery in the manager's office two days earlier under a 2 metre high pile of opened boxes and wrapping paper in the corner of the room. It was something they would never have expected to regard as highly valuable, but times had changed. There, neatly crated in a pile in the corner of the room were over 300 large bottles of mineral water. This gave them an immense feeling of happiness and satisfaction. In the town there was no reliable, clean water source. The River Ribble was the cleanest looking water available, and that could have been, and probably was, polluted by the excreta of every animal upstream, and lots of bodies. They had searched in all sorts of places to try to find good water and now, in their 'own' premises they found plenty. The girl who discovered the find yelled for joy so loudly that everyone else thought she must be in pain and came running. She was so excited that she mixed up all her words. She then stopped trying to explain and pointed to the new treasure.

They were about to descend on the bottles and start to reduce their contents when Nigel, the de facto leader of the group said, "Hang on! I think that we should give thanks to the giver of all things." All agreed and went silent while Nigel prayed, thanking God for this new found treasure and asking that He continue to give what was needed from day to day. He then prayed for friends and family members wherever they may be.

JID thought about Ruth and his mother who had both disappeared when the Labour Club had been attacked.

Nigel said, "Amen." The rest joined in with the "Amen," and Nigel then invited them to drink all they could, but by then several of them were already doing so.

Food was running short again and all their old, tried methods were giving less food. They were still getting some meat from the farm, but the vegetables had all been eaten. They felt low, but not defeated. However, they knew that they would need to find other sources of food or they would not be able to cope for long.

They were relaxing, some reading, some talking. JID was playing chess against his father in a game that would not be completed.

A violent shock wave shook the building. Some of the polystyrene tiles from the false ceiling of the supermarket fell. The chess board was thrown several feet. Supermarket shelves collapsed. Rick, one of JID's forage team got a painful blow to the head and Andrea, who had discovered the water fell, and hurt a leg.

Nigel took stock of the situation quickly and called everyone together. They had a quick count and found, to their relief that all were alive and with no mortal wounds.

. . . . .

Few realised the cause of the earthquake, but everyone on earth felt it. The explosions in the Middle East had caused a chain reaction, which rattled every fault line on earth. The Skipton fault, which had caused a few hardly noticeable tremors in northern England over the centuries suddenly sprung into life and was the main cause of the earthquake that hit Preston with a force as large as the huge quake that hit northern Pakistan in October 2005.

As the group in Preston came to their senses they decided that they would be safer out of the building in case of aftershocks. The nurse stayed outside the supermarket with the injured in a space that was reasonably well hidden, but was free from the likelihood of danger from falling wreckage.

The others went out in two groups to see if there were any casualties who they may be able to help, and report back to the injured group in three hours.

JID's group had been away for nearly half an hour when he saw a casualty. They were a hundred metres from Preston prison, whose walls had been badly damaged. A dazed, scantily clad female was climbing through a gap in the walls. JID and his team quickened their pace to a fast walk, but suddenly JID started to run as if his life depended on it! He recognised Ruth!

He caught up to her and held her so close. Both had tears of joy streaming from their eyes. JID looked closer at Ruth and saw the signs of brutality that had almost destroyed her frail body. Joy and love were momentarily displaced by a loathing and hatred for the ones that had done this to Ruth. JID asked what had happened to her, but she was more concerned for the others who were still inside the prison.

JID decided that three of the group should return to their current base near the supermarket to report back, while the others should stay with Ruth and do what they could in the prison, being guided by her to the areas that mattered most.

They approached the prison very warily after a prayer for guidance, not knowing if the self-appointed guards would be around, if they were armed and how the guards would react if they spotted outsiders in the prison. For their protection they carried stones and sticks that were there for the taking in the damaged prison.

They walked through the Victorian prison and, try as they might, were unable to make any progress without every footprint echoing throughout the prison. They had only just entered the building when they heard footsteps approaching them. JID and the men pushed in front of Ruth and braced themselves for a contest.

Ruth saw the strong woman in a Megatrade uniform and shouted, "Relax, men! She's a Friend!"

JID glanced at Ruth with an expression which said, "Have you taken leave of your senses?"

Ruth called out, "Eva, we're here!" and ran to the centre of the walkway. Eva met Ruth at the centre and gave her a hug. Then Ruth introduced JID and the others.

Ruth asked which guards were still in the prison, and Eva said that the other guards had all left immediately after the earthquake. Eva said, "I never had keys for most of the prison, but only for the torture rooms I used."

At that JID leapt towards her and kneed her to the floor, holding a brick very close to her head. Ruth pushed JID as hard as she could and said, "Stop, you don't understand! We'll tell you all about it later, but believe me, she IS a friend!"

JID stepped away from Eva, but treated her with great caution. Eva explained that she did not know where the cell keys were, but, because the other guards had left so quickly, it was likely that they would be able to find them in one of the prison offices. The offices were near to, but not in, the cell blocks. The group separated to search the offices, feeling that they were racing against time before the return of the guards. After just a few minutes one of the group shouted, "I think I've found them!"

One of the team went outside to look for the other group members. After a very short briefing they went inside to help opening the cells. Seventy five of those taken in had survived. Physically most were just shadows of their former selves. Emotionally they were confused. Spiritually they were closer to the Lord than ever and were strong as oxen in the ways that mattered most. Most were able to walk very slowly towards their new premises. Eva carried one of the prisoners whose leg muscles were, for now at least, paralysed by the treatment she had received. Others were carried a few blocks from the prison so that guards would not see them if they returned.

When all were away from the prison the basic medical care team went into overdrive. They stayed with the injured group giving pain killers from the Megatrade store, doing physiotherapy and tending wounds as well as they were able to with the supplies they had.

One of the carts towed by a horse had just arrived from the country. It was soon pressed into service as an ambulance, taking the most badly wounded to the Megatrade building. Work continued until late into the evening. The bed linen department of Megatrade had been having a sale to get rid of the previous year's stock, and had already brought the new year's stock. That provided all the bed linen they needed, but the furniture department only had twenty beds.

The tired horse obediently kept working as they ferried beds from the former buildings to the area near the new one. It was given a well-earned day off the following day.

The beds were placed outside the building because of fear of aftershocks. People kept their clothes (and whatever they could find in Megatrade) on and covered themselves with layers of blankets against the cold of the November night. Mercifully, it didn't rain that night.

After four days the aftershocks had died down and they moved the beds into the aisles of Megatrade. Teams of workers (the original 17 and the fittest of the former prisoners) moved the beds inside, getting the last one under cover five minutes before an unseasonal thunderstorm struck.

. . . . .

Nobody realised the scale of the troubles. The nuclear shock in the Middle East didn't just shake Preston.

As the violent vibrations travelled around the world so did the earthquakes. Every inch of land was shaken like a leaf in a gale. The shocks also caused tidal waves up to 30 metres high to flow and rebound round the earth for days. The main effects were felt in the Mediterranean, Indian and South Pacific oceans, but southern parts of NWE were flooded, sometimes up to five metres deep.

Every volcano on Earth that had erupted in the last 500 years erupted now, filling the air with the pungent smell of sulphur. Some volcanos that had been dormant for thousands of years also erupted, including two in north Wales, six in Scotland, two in the Lake District, one in Cornwall and one in the Pennines.

The core of the Earth had been ripped apart.

# Chapter 12. December.
## The End of the Beginning...

There was a strange atmosphere! There seemed to be no sense to life yet the ones in the supermarket looked forward with anticipation. JID and the others were beginning to get on top of the situation in the Megatrade building. Some casualties from the prison were still suffering badly and at least four were expected to carry their injuries for life without further improvement. Three of them would never be able to walk again. Most, however, had greatly improved in the fortnight since they were released from the prison. Their improvement meant that they were able to help out with more of the tasks of daily living, and the 17, who had worked like slaves, were able to share their work with more of the ones who had been in prison.

JID, Ruth and Nigel had been able to recruit a few others into a new chess club! JID played chess, and sometimes went outside with other reasonably fit younger people to kick around one of the footballs from the recreation section of the supermarket.

They were not at war with anyone, yet knew that at any moment some hostile group could arrive and turn the situation into a battlefield.

Older people talked about lots of things, yet usually returned to the same subjects after an hour or two, since the usual topics that they had discussed in previous times made no sense now. Who cares which quiz contestant won the last edition of Shootafact? The last professional football matches seemed to have been decades ago. The News (previously sponsored by Livershop) may have been happening out there, but who could know - and who cared?

Food had often seemed to be running short, yet there had always been enough when it mattered.

The surprising thing about this situation was that the people in the Megatrade building (ironically a symbol of all that was wrong with society previously) felt no boredom, or fear, or misgivings. It was as if they knew something would happen so that they would be able to break free from whatever had held them - they just didn't know quite what or when.

. . . . .

Julia Crompton and her thugs continued to plot and scheme to get back some of the power that had slipped away during the earthquake. After a few days of planning their future they had some ideas of a possible way forward. They decided that, since there were human bodies near the prison, they would be able to use them as food. The very mention of the idea was enough to make some of them vomit, so the idea was shelved until the next plan began to materialise.

. . . . .

The thugs who had tried to battle with Red Young's group when they had returned to Preston with plenty of meat were already into cannibalism! They justified it in their own minds by thinking that after they died someone might as well eat them. Anyway, it wasn't going to hurt the one they were eating.

The first person to provide a meal for them had been the girl who had been killed in the riot to get at the food that Red's group had left for them.

Later they joined with two other similar groups, which made them stronger against possible attack from outside. They realised that they were without any accepted leader, but didn't have any idea of what to do or how to organise themselves as they had been caught up in the mindlessness produced by total Company domination in the previous few years.

Their world was going to change, yet again, by a group that offered them leadership, weapons and food.

They were, as usual, armed with assorted weapons, such as slings and makeshift swords and clubs, when they were met by a smaller, but much more strongly-armed force. They were south of Preston and walking towards the town, when they heard gunshots. They started to flee in the opposite direction, then heard gunshots in front of them. Whichever way they turned there seemed to be gunmen. One sat down on the ground with her hands up, and the others followed.

A dozen gunmen broke cover, went to the group and disarmed them. Then Julia Crompton took off her mask and sat with them to do a charm offensive. She took off her uniform to reveal a figure-hugging suit of thermal underwear showing off her still impressive figure, and all the men in the thug-group immediately took notice. "I never like uniforms," she said. "They are hot and uncomfortable.

"Now, down to business," she continued. "We have a group of fit and able people who are able to give stability to your world."

"What's dability?" said Bill, one of the thugs, speaking for all of them. One of the effects of the last few years was that the language of most people had rapidly degraded.

Julia realised that she would need to speak in very basic English. "We want the world to work well, and you can help us to do that. Where did you sleep last night?" she asked.

One pointed and said, "In those woods. We kept close to stay warm. I lay close to Starry-By. She's nice."

"We can give you proper beds! Inside buildings! And lots to eat! We are busy. There's lots to do. If you help us to do some of the work you can live with us."

"Can me and Starry- By share a bed?" he asked, grinning.

"Yes, I will make sure that you can."

"OK!" He said. "I'n't it, ev'ryone?"

They all grunted approvingly and nodded. Then they started to walk towards their new job - preparing human bodies for themselves and their new leaders to eat in Preston prison. Bill thought the idea was very funny and kept making stupid jokes about manburgers!

The general mood in the prison was one of dejection and hopelessness. Both Julia and her team shared the same emotions as their new assistants. They couldn't figure out what they were doing or why they were doing it. Many had considered suicide, but they feared death even more than they loathed this miserable life.

. . . . .

There were a few survivors of the armies that had been camped at Meggido. Most had been wounded, or badly burned. They were all suffering from radiation sickness. They, like the groups of thugs near Preston, were trying to decide whether they should look after themselves or group together to find and use whatever food and resources were available.

They had all tried to get nearer to the blasts in the hope of finding food or other resources, but realised that the whole area was nothing more than scorched earth.

They tried to go south, but the Israeli army had placed a cordon about 30 kilometres north of Jerusalem, and their efficient military machine was easily able to withstand a handful of dazed men from the battle zone. The only people allowed to cross the cordon were Israeli passport holders.

Jerusalem had been shaken, but not stirred. A lot of buildings had collapsed due to bombs and earthquakes, but the basic infrastructure had survived better than in any other country on earth. Their civil defence network had most of the daily needs of life available and they coped as they always had.

It was mid-afternoon when the action started. Life was continuing in Israel. The food situation was bad, but not as bad as in many places on earth. Little in the previous few months had been predictable, and it is certain that nobody expected this!

At around midday the whole Earth heard irregular rumblings, as lumps of something came out of the ground and ascended. Many, but by no means all, ascended from past and present cemetery sites. Some of the bundles were neatly shaped and others more randomly shaped. As they rose into the air they began to reshape.

The Israeli air force was scrambled as a precaution at the first sight of whatever it was. After the recent happenings at Meggido they could afford no mistakes. When they got nearer to the UFOs they began to report back. "Action Flyer to base: It seems that there are a great number of UFO's, could be thousands of them. They seem to be thin and roundish, with the longest dimension from top to bottom. The vertical dimensions seem to vary between about one and two metres high and one at the centre is blindingly bright. They are ascending slowly. There is no reading on the radioactivity scale so they will not be carrying nukes. They seem to be centring on a UFO that is descending over Jerusalem. I'm sure that my feelings are irrational, but I am terrified. Request further orders."

The pilot had flown over several hostile areas in the past and been successful in three mid-air dogfights. In each one he had shown nerves of steel, and had only a slightly higher than usual heartrate. Now his monitor showed a heartrate of 163 beats each minute.

"Take no action at this stage," came the reply to his request. "Only fire if there is a clear risk of hostile action. I will be contacting the Government to get the political angle on this. Meanwhile approach cautiously, keep an eye on the situation and keep me posted.

The aircraft got about 500 metres closer and then, whatever the pilot tried to do, the plane turned round to face in the opposite direction. He turned the plane again, and again got no nearer than about 4 kilometres before the plane turned and flew away from the descending figure. He reported this to base, who sent out a message on all frequencies asking for the vessels to report back and declare their intentions. A second message was sent out, that if the Israeli air traffic control received no message their presence would be treated as hostile and Israel would take any action it deemed necessary. That message would always be acted upon if the aircraft was friendly.

On the ground there were mixed emotions. By now all the people in a large area round Jerusalem had heard about the occurrence and gone outside to see for themselves. Most were terrified, but some were quietly confident that they had been waiting for this for a long time.

The order to fire was sent to the fighter. The pilot duly fired, but his weapons failed and not a single projectile went anywhere near the target. This type of missile had been deadly in battles so far, but now they slowly slid out of their cases and dropped towards the ground.

. . . . .

The soldiers just outside the 30 kilometre exclusion zone could see that there was something happening near Jerusalem. Then every man's mini 3Dvid started to speak. It was not in a language they recognised, but they could all understand every word. They sat, open mouthed and in fear. "We have an important announcement from Jerusalem that will affect every person on earth...

· · · · ·

The tension in the prison had been growing all day, even though they seemed to have got over any initial misgivings they may have had concerning their food and its processing. The 3Dvid sprung into life. "We have an important announcement from Jerusalem that will affect every person on earth. This was prophesied in several different ways in the pages of the Bible...

· · · · ·

In the supermarket everyone knew that something special was going to happen today. There was a happy party atmosphere. They were recharging their glasses with bottled water and feasting from recently discovered tins of fancy biscuits. Mirabel was diabetic and was banned from having anything sweet. When she saw the biscuits she glanced at the nurse and said she intended to eat her fill as today was going to be so different. "Yes, you're right!" said the nurse. Then the 3Dvid started. Out of all of the 3Dvids in the store, the biggest and best switched itself on. (They had no idea how, there was no electrical power available. This was a different kind of power!)

"We have an important announcement from Jerusalem which will affect every person on earth. This was prophesied in several different ways in the pages of the Bible. As promised, Jesus Christ has returned with faithful people from the past and has come here to collect his faithful people still alive. Those who have chosen and been selected will be able to enter the joy of the Lord...

There was a huge cheer from everyone in the store! This was what they were waiting for! As they gathered round the 3Dvid they realised that the image didn't just stay in the room but went completely through the ceiling and into the clear sky above the shop. Somehow the picture in the store had outgrown the building and sent it's picture way beyond.

The cheering in the supermarket seemed as loud as anything the crowd at Preston North End football ground could have produced! JID held Ruth's hand and his father's. The rest joined hands to make a ring. The ones desperately injured in bed were able to get up and join the fun. They danced around the 3Dvid, and then caught sight of the figure at the centre high above them, with thousands at his side.

. . . . .

In Preston prison the 3Dvid continued, "We have an important announcement from Jerusalem that will affect every person on earth. This was prophesied in several different ways in the pages of the Bible. As promised, Jesus Christ has returned with faithful people from the past and has come here to collect his faithful people. Those who have chosen and been selected will be able to enter the joy of the Lord. Those not selected have left it too late and will suffer for every sin.

Starry-By shouted, "That's not fair. I want to be nice."

Julie cursed about the 3Dvid announcement and said that nobody could threaten her. She grabbed Starry-By's boyfriend, holding a dagger at his throat. She said that if anyone moved she would kill him. In her own mind she was trying to show anyone who may try to harm her that she was even more evil than the attackers, and that they would have to face the consequences.

She didn't realise that she was dealing with the One who had chosen to be overpowered. but would never do so again.

. . . . .

The men in the exclusion zone North of Jerusalem heard their 3Dvids. "We have an important announcement from Jerusalem that will affect every person on earth. This was prophesied in several different ways in the pages of the Bible. As promised, Jesus Christ has returned with faithful people from the past and has come here to collect his faithful people. Those who have chosen and been selected will be able to enter the joy of the Lord. Those not selected have left it too late and will suffer for every sin. It is appointed for mortal humans to die once, and after that the judgement…

Many froze at the thought. They had heard a similar message from a parent, a teacher or a church leader in their own lands, but they had found it an inconvenience when they had important life decisions to make. Now they realised that they had made the wrong choice when it mattered most.

. . . . .

In Jerusalem they had no 3Dvids operating - they were not needed there, but they heard the voice loud and clear, "We have an important announcement that will affect every person on earth. This was prophesied in several different ways in the pages of the Bible. As promised, Jesus Christ has returned with faithful people from the past and has come here to collect today's faithful people. Those who have chosen and been selected will be able to enter the joy of the Lord. It is appointed for mortal humans to die once, and after that the judgement. God's Son came to his own people, and his own people did not accept him. But to all who received him, who believed in his name, he gave power to become children of God..."

As in most places on Earth, most of the people were filled with dread. However, from some parts of the city the sounds of joy were as clear as in the Preston supermarket! As the figure at the centre descended, the ones who were making the joyful sounds were overcome by a joy that even they had not experienced before.

They had been through the hard times of the last few years and especially the last few months but they had remained faithful to the true Hope of Israel, Jesus Christ. Now they would be the first surviving people to meet Him. They were looking upwards with hope in their hearts, when they felt the weight on their feet reducing and they were carried into the air to meet their Saviour.

. . . . .

The Preston Christians were watching the extended 3Dvid that seemed to extend right through the supermarket roof, when they too felt their feet leaving the floor. They rose at a great speed and automatically held their hands over their heads as they expected to hit the roof. That didn't happen as they continued to ascend and seemingly become part of the 3Dvid picture. In a moment or two they realised that they WERE part of the picture - and a very important part.

They knew that they were now part of the great prophesy, and were going to be with the Lord. They knew that people who had rejected Him had no further chance of selection. When judgement happened that group would be found guilty.

JID knew that he would, like all mankind, be found guilty, but, unlike most, he would be treated as perfect! He reflected on the words of Jesus, that he heard from his Father-in-Law at their second or third meeting and he had since learned by heart, 'God loved the world so much that he gave His one and only Son, so that whoever believes on Him shall not perish, but have eternal life. God didn't send His Son into the world to condemn the world, but to save the world through Him. Whoever believes in Him is not condemned, but whoever does not believe stands condemned already, because they have not believed in the name of God's one and only Son.

. . . . .

All over the world most people remained firmly attached to the ground. They knew that they were facing something that would be so much worse than they had seen or experienced before. All hope had been extinguished. They had not accepted Jesus Christ and had no way of successfully making any plea for inclusion. They were rejected, and it had been their own choice!

. . . . .

One of God's greatest gifts to mankind had been individuality. In the whole of the history of the earth no two people, even 'identical' twins, had identical personalities. All had been able to make individual choices. Each had been special.

As JID was getting closer and closer to the One at the centre, it occurred to him that he was still himself – and was not part of some kind of blob of combined consciousness. That gift of individuality and personality was still an important part of him. The only difference was that his rebellion, which had still been in the background on Earth, and which he had occasionally shown even recently, had vanished with the complete joy of togetherness with God.

He felt himself moving slightly forward, towards Jesus at the centre of the huge airborne crowd . He got to within less than a metre of Jesus, who looked him in the eye and smiled. "Well done, Good and Faithful Servant. You are entering the joy of Your Lord. There are millions of millions of people here, but I am available to each one at every moment. We will be together in the New Jerusalem."

JID was in a state of bliss, even greater than his most intimate moments with Ruth, yet this was not the same as the kind of love that he had had before. It was something much greater. He looked up and, to one side, he could see mountains with a city in the middle. It was all slightly blurred. There was a splashing sound as he flew out of water and came to rest on the shore a few metres from Ruth, his father and some friends. Suddenly he shouted, "Red! It's great to see you! How long have you been here?"

"I got here about ten seconds before you did!" he replied. "It's great, isn't it!"

JID looked round and, within about 20 metres, were the Christians who had been such a special part of his life over the last year, including his parents, Ruth and her parents, Kit and all the others from the Chess Club, the pubs, the labour clubs and the supermarket.

He then spotted Kenneth Kippam and Eva who were standing near each other. He ran towards them. "Kenneth, er, Fred and Eva! I owe each of you a huge apology. Please forgive me!"

Simultaneously Keith said, "JID, I'm sorry for everything I did to you!" and Eva said, "I am the one who needs forgiving."

They put their arms round each other and wept buckets! These were not tears of pain, but of forgiveness. This was an extra gift of forgiveness, as if they needed any more. These sins had already been put right, but they enjoyed a bonus when they expressed forgiveness for each other.

. . . . .

Soon after the great meeting of friends, the initial excitement gave way to an awesome silence. They saw a dazzling white throne. It was at a distance, yet they could take in every detail. The excitement was silent, but gripping. Everyone there was overtaken by the joy and the expectation of the whole event. Then a voice spoke in the language that they had heard earlier and, again, everyone understood every word and emotion it conveyed. The voice declared:

> 'See, the home of God is among mortals.
> He will dwell with them;
> they will be his peoples,
> and God himself will be with them;
> He will wipe every tear from their eyes.
> Death will be no more;
> mourning and crying and pain will be no more,
> for the first things have passed away.'

JID could hardly take it all in. As he was enjoying the whole scene, and praising God with voice, mind and spirit, he again felt light and felt God's amazing presence. Then he felt himself being lifted up. The previous restrictions held him no longer! He saw the city that had been booked for everyone in the huge crowd of millions. It was absolutely vast - big enough for everyone involved. Yet unlike the huge cities of earlier days, like London or Karachi, the atmosphere was not noisy and fume filled, but was utterly peaceful. People in it would make a noise in praise to God, but would never do anything to upset or disrupt another person. They would have all the transport they needed without cost and without pollution.

He saw that everything was as pure and joyful as he had ever imagined - and more so. There was just one thing missing. He called out, "But God, where is the Church? There must be a Church (or a lot of them.) Perhaps a huge cathedral or temple."

Jesus came alongside him and said, "You are in it! You do not need a special building. In the past you worshipped in all kinds of places and each became special to you. You do not need a special building here, because I am here with the Father and the Spirit of God. You are always in the centre of worship. "Come with me, there is a lot more to see…"

JID's feet touched the surface once again. Jesus and JID walked into the mountains and came to a stream. The sky was as clear as crystal and everything was well lit, yet he couldn't see the sun or moon. He asked why.

"When I was on Earth I was the Light of the World. People didn't see me as a shining light, but with the eyes of faith and a knowledge of my word I shone and enlightened their deepest understanding. Now I and my Father are the light of Heaven. No other light is needed.

JID realised that the light of the skies was just a reflection of God, the Father and Son. The Spirit, who had drawn people to Jesus in the first place, was there and still working in people. He continued to give them joy and peace (as He had down the ages) but now these qualities were uninterrupted by human sin, which had finished for ever.

Jesus showed him a river that ran through the city and invited him to have a drink. It was water, but again not like he had tasted before. It seemed to give him an even greater grasp of life and reality than he had ever realised earlier, yet this was no drug. Like everything else around it had a real purity and, like everything else, would have been almost impossible to enjoy by imperfect people. Now the people in God's presence had been perfected and they were for the first time able to enjoy perfection without feeling impure.

"What kind of water is that?" gasped JID. "Water of life!" said Jesus. "You were alive on earth. You grasped a vision of greater life when you accepted my work in your life. Now you have grasped it fully, and this water represents it. JID sat by the river and took handfuls of it. He remembered taking beautiful water from a highland stream against his parents' advice when they were enjoying a holiday in Scotland when he was 12-years old. It tasted wonderful, but he had stomach problems for the next three days. There was no fear this time. There was no sickness here. It had been destroyed in the way that sickness had previously destroyed people.

JID was shown his part of the city, with his friends around him, yet he knew that there were millions of people there and they all had special stories of faith and hope. There were stories of last minute conversions. There were stories of faith through suffering, and so much more.

He looked in the face of Jesus and asked if he could meet some extraordinary Christians. The reply was, "They are all extraordinary, and you will have time to meet them all. You will be able to enjoy football and chess, and games never invented on Earth. You will be able to enjoy and learn. You will be able to expand your mind and your experience, but all in good time. You will also be able to worship."

At that comment, JID fell on his knees and worshipped for a long time. (He had no idea how long, but that didn't matter. He wanted to give the glory to the Three-in-One who had made it all possible.

JID then got to his feet and saw that he was near his friends.

JID was overcome by emotions he had never imagined. Eventually he recovered enough to speak, mumbling like a child. "That was amazing! It was Jesus! He was talking to me! ME! He told me all about the city. The things we could do! We can meet the giants of faith! All of them! We can enjoy things on earth and we can worship Him. Jesus spent hours with ME! It must have been the whole afternoon! He did that for ME!

Together the rest chorused, "That's what He did for us!"

They laughed, they wept for joy, they had that peace that the world had never been able to replicate.

It was all that they could possibly have wanted or expected - and so much more.

CPSIA information can be obtained at www.ICGtesting.com
Printed in the USA
LVOW01s1920171214

419291LV00033B/1033/P